The Voyage of the Pegasus II

The Return of the Cobra

written and illustrated by

Eliza Crooks

ISBN 979-8-218-39907-8

"Beware; for I am fearless, and therefore powerful."
-Mary Shelley

To All of My Teachers Throughout the Years

Foreword

Before I even finished *The Voyage of the Pegasus*, I was already beginning to plan this sequel. This book not only answers previous questions from the original, but also leaves new questions for the reader. It introduces three new characters: Michael, Sydney's sweet and loving boyfriend, Ginger, a timid, but caring eight-year-old, and Jerry, Sydney's pet ferret. This sequel also puts a bigger emphasis on Dylan.

As I have matured since my last book, *The Voyage of the Pegasus II* dives deeper into true love, purpose, sacrifice, and trust. I have poured my own emotions and experiences into this story. Ideally, I want this book to touch both the reader's mind and heart. Yes, I'm still young and still learning, but I have also devoted my time, energy, and effort to my sequel. I have enjoyed writing this compelling story, and I hope you enjoy it, too!

Eliza Crooks

Table of Contents

A New Recruit and a New Beginning

It was November in the year of 1694. I had just turned fourteen, but the days hadn't seemed to grow from the time I had become the heir to Pedro Francisco. I still felt like a young and adventurous teenager, but I was happier, as though I had been freed from the chains of anxiety wrapped around me. As I came into London's harbor, I felt as though it was May again, but much colder. I dropped the anchor and looked back, as I saw Ryker come up onto the deck through the fog.

"Hey," he said.

"Hey," I replied.

"You remember this harbor, don't you?" Ryker asked.

"Yeah, of course, I do," I said. "This is where we first kissed, how could I possibly forget?"

"You know, this is also where we first met," Ryker said.

"Oh right," I said. "I started screaming at you to get on the ship, and you did, willingly, and I liked you the whole time without knowing it."

"He knows, he was there," Sawyer scoffed as he climbed up from below deck.

"Do you mind?" I asked.

"Ryker, Alice is chasing me because I took all of her gold, but I'm getting tired of being chased, so I need you to run her off," Sawyer said.

"I'm not gonna run off an eight-year-old for you," Ryker said.

"Why can't you just give her stuff back?" I suggested.

"Because that would mean I surrendered to a girl who's two years younger than me," Sawyer argued.

"Well, then, the joke's on you," Ryker said.

"Let me settle this real quick," I said. "I need you to roll up the sails."

"Okay," Ryker said, as he kissed my cheek. Sawyer rolled his eyes. I followed him below deck to his room, where he had stashed the stolen gold.

Alice suddenly jumped out from under Ryker's hammock, tackled Sawyer, and screamed, "Give it back! Give it back, or you'll pay!"

"Belle, help!" Sawyer pleaded.

"Wait, I wanna see what *pay* means," I laughed.

"It means this!" Alice proclaimed as she held up a bottle of Sydney's perfume.

"No! Don't! Please!" Sawyer begged.

"And it's even the lavender kind," Alice threatened.

"No!" Sawyer cried.

"Where's my gold?" Alice asked.

"I'm not telling you!" Sawyer whined.

"Fine, then," Alice said, as she took the lid off of the perfume bottle, and poured it into Sawyer's face.

"Oh my gosh, why does Sydney's perfume smell that strong?" I coughed.

"Blah! I got all in my mouth and everything! I'm gonna smell like a girl for a week," Sawyer complained.

"Perfect for a boy who screams like a girl," Alice teased.

"Hey! I'll have you know that I have one chest hair!" Sawyer said.

"And I'll cut it off if you don't give me back my gold!" Alice threatened.

"Who wasted all of my perfume?" Sydney scolded.

"She did it," I said, as I pointed to Alice.

"Yeah, but Sawyer started it," Alice said.

"I don't care, I want my perfume back," Sydney said.

"And I want my gold back," Alice whined.

"And I want my sanity back, but we can't always get what we want, can we?" I said sarcastically.

"Well, I don't care," Sydney said. "All I want right now is to see Michael and go to the Royal Ball and wear a pretty dress and..."

"*Squawk!* Sydney's getting married! Sydney's getting married!" Donna flew into Sawyer and Ryker's room.

"No one is getting married," I clarified.

"Then why is she gonna wear a pretty dress? I've heard much about human weddings, and this sounds like one to me," Donna squawked.

"Remember, Donna, how Michael asked me to the ball back in May?" Sydney said.

"*Squawk!* Nope!" Donna replied.

"Hey, Sawyer, some dumb-looking guy in the harbor wants you," Ryker said as he walked into his room. "There's a girl with him. I don't know what they want."

"What?" Sawyer asked as he got up from the floor, with no idea what was happening. Everyone followed him up to the deck to find the strange sight of a British noble and a young girl in a simple black dress. Her bonnet covered two French braids and shaded her blue eyes.

"Oh, um, hello," I started, not really knowing what to say. "I'm Belle Smith..."

"I couldn't care less," the noble scoffed. "Where is Sawyer Anderson?"

"Here," Sawyer said. "I'm here."

"Good," the noble said. "This is Ginger Anderson, your eight-year-old step-sister. She..."

"She can speak for herself, that's what," I interrupted, already annoyed just by the sight of a noble.

"Wait," Sawyer said. "She's *what?*"

"Never mind," the noble said. "Ginger, tell the strange children of your plight."

"Well... um... okay," Ginger said. "So, um, my father died when I was young and, and my mother married your father, Peter Anderson. And he always talked about you... he loved you a lot. And he told me about how you were lost during the storm. So, um, my mother died six months ago of leukemia. And, and then your father had a heart attack two months ago. He... he knew he was dying, so he told me that you had ended up on a ship with a Pegasus on it and that there had been talk of the same ship in London. News had made it to the New World that the pirates on this ship had somehow been invited to the Royal Ball, so I was sent here."

The entire crew was baffled. This was one of the oddest events I had ever witnessed, especially after thinking of how Sawyer must have felt. I could tell he was about to cry. I knew he loved his father and wouldn't take the news well, but his response was nothing like I'd expected. After hesitating Sawyer finally said, "You're not my sister."

"Well, not your real sister," Ginger said. "I'm your step..."

"No, you're not my real sister, you're not my step-sister, and you're not welcome in my family. Get away from me," Sawyer said. Sawyer ran into his room and Ryker followed him. Ginger watched them leave and suddenly burst into tears.

"Well, it seems as though you have no family left after all," the noble said. "To the orphanage, we go."

"Ugh, do you ever know when to shut up?" I asked the noble. I grabbed Ginger and said, "I'll take her."

"Maybe I should just send you to the orphanage, too," he said.

"Maybe you should just give me the girl, and beat it," I snapped.

"What authority do you have over me or the girl?" he asked.

"Well, I have a brain, and you don't," I argued.

"Are you going to give me a lot of trouble, if you don't get what you want?"

"Yes."

"Fine," the noble said. "Just take her and get out of my hair."

The snobbish noble let go of Ginger and walked away. Ginger looked at me and softly asked, "Why did you do that?"

"Because I'm not gonna let you live all alone in an orphanage when you could be here with us," I answered.

"But the only family I have left hates me," Ginger sobbed. "Can't you see that I'm not welcome here?"

"But you *are* welcome here," Sydney said.

"No, I'm not," Ginger said. "I just don't know what I did wrong. Sawyer only ever knew me for two minutes. I just don't understand."

"It's not you," I said. "Sawyer's a good kid, he just needs some time and he'll warm up to you. His brain processes things wrong sometimes. No, his brain is wrong most of the time. But for now, just make yourself at home in my room, right over there."

"Okay, I will, if that's okay," Ginger said, as she dried her tears.

Sawyer suddenly came up from below deck. "I left something up here," he said, but became angry when he saw Ginger. "What are you still doing here? I thought I told you that you weren't welcome."

Ginger began to cry again and ran into my room. I looked at Sawyer and said, "Who do you think you are? You are the only family she has left, and you won't even give her a chance."

"Sawyer, get down here," Ryker said from below deck. "We need to talk. Right now." Ryker grabbed Sawyer and pulled him into their cabin room. I went to talk to Ginger, who was still in tears.

Ryker let go of Sawyer and asked him, "How, on Earth, could you treat that girl the way you did? She has lost everything, and you turned her down on the spot. I don't know if you feel replaced or you're just upset about the whole thing, but this just isn't like you. So go ahead, start talking."

"It's not my fault! She ruined my life!" Sawyer argued.

"No, no, she did not ruin your life," Ryker said.

"Oh, so you just don't get it, do you? I lost my father two years ago and he meant everything to me. My mother died six years ago, too. But once I'm gone, my father just forgets about the rest of his family and decides to get a new one, because he's just given up on us! So then, this girl, my replacement, barges in saying that my father is dead. So, not only am I forgotten, but my father is dead and I have to deal with everything all at once! And it hurts me that my father didn't try harder to find me."

"But you like it here. You wanted to stay and you stopped looking for him after a few weeks. There was only so much either of you could do."

"It's not my fault we were separated!"

"I didn't say it was your fault!"

"We tried to find him but we couldn't. After some time I just decided it was a lost cause. It's not my fault!"

"I know!"

"Well, then stop saying it is!"

"I'm not, you are!"

"Well, maybe, if I'd been there for him, he wouldn't have died," Sawyer said, crying now.

"Oh," Ryker said. "So, not only do you feel replaced, but you feel at fault?"

Sawyer nodded in tears.

"Listen, your father didn't stop loving you or your mother, he just found two other people to love too. And it's not your fault your father died, it's no one's fault. Things just happen that people can't change. That being said, Ginger also lost her family, and you're all she has. Sawyer, I know what it's like to be turned down by my own family. I would hate to see you do that to someone. So when you're ready, go and talk to her. Okay?"

"Okay," Sawyer agreed.

"Sawyer?" Ryker asked.

"What?"

"Why do you smell like a girl?"

"I was harassed by an eight-year-old! The eight-year-old *you* didn't fight off," Sawyer answered.

Meanwhile, Ginger continued to cry her eyes out in my room. I felt terrible. She was too young and innocent to lose everyone she loved. I wasn't sure what to say to her, but I tried my best.

"He's not a bad kid, he's really not," I said. "He's just upset about his father. You see, the night I met him, they were separated from each other. We tried and tried to find his father, but there was just no use. Sawyer began to like being a pirate, or a sort of pirate, at least. After some time we gave up, and Sawyer just ended up staying with us. But one thing I do know is that when someone you really and truly love dies, you may try to blame someone. When I thought Ryker was dead, I blamed myself. I even tried to blame Sydney, at one point. Sawyer probably blamed himself because he gave up on going home."

"Oh," Ginger said. "I never thought he would blame himself. I just knew he'd be upset. And I know he probably feels replaced. Come to think of it, I sort of did just barge in. He wasn't wrong."

"He still shouldn't have treated you the way he did," I said. "But he will accept you, he just needs some time."

"Okay… but I know nothing about being a pirate," Ginger said, as she smiled a little for the first time that day.

"Please, you have nothing to worry about," I reassured her. "You'll catch on."

"Oh, okay," Ginger said. "But what are you doing in London?"

"Alright, so last May we were here to celebrate our victory in Lost Island… I'll tell you about that later… and there was this dork named Michael, and he decided to ask Sydney to the Royal Ball. So we're here for that. I'm not really sure how it's gonna work, us being pirates and all, but yeah. I don't want to go. I still don't think I can shove myself into a ball gown, but I'm just doing it for Sydney and Ryker, I guess."

"Is he your date?" Ginger assumed.

"Yeah, he's my boyfriend," I said. "We're both fourteen."

Suddenly, we heard a knock on the door. I opened it to find Sawyer looking upset, but not angry.

"What do you want?" I asked.

"To apologize," he answered.

"No, Sawyer, you don't have to apologize," Ginger said.

"No, I do," Sawyer said. "I should have welcomed you. You're my sister, after all." Sawyer hugged Ginger, both of them crying a little... until Alice barged in.

"Hi, I'm Alice!" she exclaimed. "I heard you were eight. I'm also eight! We should be friends. Wanna be friends? We can braid each other's hair and make bracelets and beat up Ryker. It'll be fun! Oh, and this is Sawyer. He's ten years old and a big fat doofus. And if he's ever mean to you again, you can just punch him in the guts and if he cries, you tell him to toughen up. We

15

could even be roommates and kick Sydney out. Come on, roomy!" Alice grabbed Ginger's wrist and dragged her below deck.

"Don't worry, Ginger!" I yelled. "She's a really nice girl! She won't hurt you! You're on her good side!"

And so we found our newest recruit, Ginger Anderson. An empty room was set up for Ginger and Alice to share, while Sydney kept hers to herself. Ginger was loved by all of the Stowaways and had no trouble fitting in. However, I was still worried about her. How could such a sweet little girl become a pirate?

"Alright, Belle! I bought twelve different dresses for us girls to try on, using the money you gave me. Let's get to work!" Sydney exclaimed holding a pile of dresses.

"Great," I said, as I rolled my eyes. The tragic day had come.

"Ooh! Dresses! Yay!" Ginger cheered.

"I want the pink one!" Alice said.

"We should give the pink one to Sawyer. It would suit him the best," I giggled.

"Hey! That wasn't very nice!" Sawyer argued as he appeared from below deck.

"No, she's right," Ryker said, coming up after Sawyer.

"*Squawk!* Sawyer smells like a girl! Sawyer screams like a girl! And Sawyer is shorter than an eight-year-old girl! *Squawk!*"

"Shut up, Donna," Sawyer whined.

"Don't say that to me!"

"Or what?" Sawyer asked.

"Or I'll peck your eyes out! Peck, peck..."

"Donna, just stop," I ordered.

"Yeah, Donna! Sawyer's already blind to the fact that he's a big dummy, don't make him physically blind, too!" Alice said.

"Are they always like this?" Ginger asked nervously.

"No," I said, "this is the first time Donna's ever said anything that's accurate."

"Belle! I thought you were sticking up for me!" Sawyer scolded.

"Sawyer, we're joking," Sydney said.

"*Squawk!* Speak for yourself!" Donna argued.

"Shut your little mouth!" Sawyer demanded.

"Beak! It's a beak, mind you!" Donna corrected.

"Fine, Sawyer," I said. "You're just as dumb and gross as any normal boy."

"Thank you!" Sawyer exclaimed.

"Can we please change the subject?" Ginger begged.

"Yeah, sure," Sydney said. "Girls, who wants to have a sleepover in Belle's room tonight?"

"Why does it have to be in my room?" I asked.

"Because the captain's room is the best room," Alice answered.

"Does this concern us, at all?" Sawyer asked.

"No," Sydney said.

"Great, but before we leave, Ryker and I have a complaint," Sawyer said. "There are now five girls on this ship and only two of us. That just doesn't seem fair."

"Yeah, and you and Ginger are the only girls that don't drive us insane," Ryker said.

"Well, it's not like I can just find another boy," I said.

"What about Michael?" Sydney suggested.

"Yeah, your sweet baby, Michael," Alice teased.

"*Squawk!* Sweet Baby Michael! Sweet Baby Michael!" Donna chirped.

"Yeah, Belle, go find 'Sweet Baby Michael' and bring him back here," Sawyer demanded.

"Do you expect me to kidnap him, or something?" I asked sarcastically.

"You kidnapped me, apparently," Ryker said.

"I did not kidnap you!"

"That's what you said, after Sydney destroyed your self-esteem in the Underground Passage in Lost Island," Ryker countered.

"Well, I was a hot mess at the time, so give me a break."

"Finally, someone other than Ryker calls her hot!" Sydney exclaimed.

"Again, can we please change the subject?" Ginger pleaded.

"We should go." Ryker said.

"You should," Alice agreed. "Bye, bye, now!"

"Okay, everyone be ready for our sleepover tonight at six o'clock," Sydney advised. The afternoon went by quickly, as did supper. Soon after, Alice, Ginger, and Sydney had all changed into nightgowns and settled in my room.

"Why aren't you wearing a nightgown?" Sydney asked me.

"Because I've been through enough pain already," I answered coldly.

"Well, I can see your ugly feet," Sydney complained. "Could you please do something about that?"

"At least I don't have a double-jointed toe, like you," I said.

"Please, just put those dirty dawgs away," Sydney begged.

"I can do whatever I want with my feet," I argued.

"Fine. Truth or dare?" Sydney asked.

"Can't we play something else?" I pleaded.

"Just answer the question," Alice said.

"Fine, dare," I decided.

"Let us call you Mrs. Collins for the rest of the night," Sydney said.

"Aw! Belle and Ryker Collins!" Alice exclaimed.

"But Sydney..." I started.

"No, no, no. No *buts*," Sydney insisted. "It's a dare. You have to go with it."

"But I'm the captain," I argued.

"Belle, you're ruining the game," Alice complained.

"Yeah, Mrs. Collins, you're ruining the game," Ginger agreed.

"Stop calling me that!" I demanded.

"Fine, I'll give you another dare," Sydney said. "Let me pierce your ears."

"What? No!" I shrieked.

"Oh, come on, every lady gets their ears pierced," Sydney pleaded.

"Do I look like a lady to you?" I asked.

"No, but pirates do it, too," Alice said.

"Please," Sydney begged.

"Fine, whatever," I said. Sydney ran into her room and came back with a needle and a pair of small gold hoop earrings.

"Hold still," she said.

"Why is that needle so close to my head?" I asked. "You're gonna decapitate me!"

"No, I'm not. I'm just gonna pierce your ears, now hold still."

"If I become deaf because of this, you, Sydney, will feel that shame for the rest of your... ouch! Oh, wait, that doesn't hurt."

"Hm... look at that, you're not deaf and your head is still attached to your neck," Sydney said.

"Ginger, your turn," Alice said.

"Truth," Ginger said.

"Have you ever liked a boy?" Alice inquired.

"Boys are gross," Ginger answered. "No."

"Sawyer's not…" Alice started.

"You like Sawyer?" I screamed. "Alright, then, I dare you to kiss him!"

"I don't like Sawyer, we're just friends," Alice argued.

"Yeah, that's exactly what Belle said a year ago when I caught her flirting with Ryker," Sydney said.

"We were, at the time!" I said.

"Wait, who am I?" Sydney asked. "Hey, babe. I'm a dork and you're the only girl who's ever loved me. I think you're hot and worth fighting your ex-captain for. Now, I shall run into the snaky tunnel of death…"

"Ryker's not a dork!" I cried.

"Yes, he is," Alice said.

"He saved our lives!" I argued.

"Fine, fine," Sydney said. "I'll give you that one."

"Thank you," I said. "Now, Alice, go kiss Sawyer. If you do, I'll give you whatever you want."

Alice got up and ran into Sawyer's room. The three of us followed her excitedly. Alice kicked open the door, grabbed Sawyer, and declared, "Sawyer, I'm doing this on a dare. I don't love you, and I never, ever, ever will!"

And at that, Alice kissed Sawyer... on his *elbow*. I instantly died laughing. Sawyer and Alice's faces became bright red.

"Sawyer... do you have a secret girlfriend?" Ryker teased.

"No!" Sawyer denied it, as he pushed Alice away and asked her, "What is your problem?"

"Oh, please, any girl dumb enough to like you has serious problems," Alice retorted, as she pushed past us to go back to my room.

"Whose idea was that?" Sawyer inquired.

"No one's," I said abruptly, as I darted out of the room. Ginger and Sydney followed behind.

As we entered my room, I greeted Alice saying, "Hello, Mrs. Anderson!"

"I think I deserve my pay," Alice said as she looked through the scope of a pistol.

"You can't give her a gun!" Ginger shrieked.

"Fine, Alice, you can have the gun, as long as you promise not to fire it when there are people around, or inside. I don't want the ship sinking because you blew a hole in it," I said.

"Gee, thanks!" Alice exclaimed.

"Just don't let Sawyer have it," Sydney warned. "I'll bet you everything I own he'll point it the wrong way and accidentally shoot himself."

"Ooh, good point," Alice agreed, as she tucked the pistol away.

"Hey... look at all these dresses I brought. How about we try them on?" Sydney hinted.

"How 'bout we don't?" I objected.

"Come on, Belle, stop being a party pooper," Sydney pleaded.

"But dresses are tight and itchy, and I'll trip on the skirt."

"I call dibs on the pink one!" Alice exclaimed as she snatched a vibrant pink dress from Sydney and slipped it on.

"You look like a princess!" Ginger complimented.

"I know," Alice agreed with a curtsy.

"Belle, put this on," Sydney demanded as she tossed me a rose-gold dress.

"But I don't want to," I whined.

"Please, Belle, do it for me, your *best friend*," Sydney begged.

"Whatever," I grumbled, as I tried on the dress. It was definitely beautiful, with elegant flowers intricately sewn onto the rose gold fabric. However, the dress was indeed tight, itchy, and very, very annoying.

"Belle! Look at you! You're gorgeous!" Sydney exclaimed.

"I hate this dress," I grunted.

"But it's so pretty," Ginger said.

"I can't move my arms," I complained.

"Yes you can," Sydney argued. "Toughen up."

"Excuse me?" I said. "*You're* telling *me* to toughen up? I don't think so!"

"I think you both need to toughen up," Alice retorted. "Or am I the only mature one on this ship?"

"Mature? Mature? You are not mature, little missy!" Sydney said.

"Who does Belle trust with a pistol? Not you!" Alice bragged.

"I trust Sydney!" I disagreed.

"M-hm." Alice rolled her eyes.

"Didn't you say you had a parrot? Where is she?" Ginger asked.

"She's in a better place now," Alice answered, as she patted Ginger's shoulder.

"Oh… I'm sorry," Ginger said, completely believing Alice. "How did she die?"

"She was murdered," Alice replied gravely.

"She's in the cargo hold," I clarified.

"You kept her body?" Ginger squealed.

"No, *someone* just likes to make up stories," Sydney said.

"Who could that be?" Alice asked, with red cheeks and a sheepish grin.

At length, Ginger scolded, "Alice, you lied to me, you… liar!"

"I was only joking," Alice said. "I'm surprised you believed that."

"Stop being mean to the new girl," I said.

"I will teach you my ways," Alice promised Ginger.

"Please don't," Ginger said nervously.

"Here, I'll demonstrate," Alice said, walking toward Sydney.

"Or we could give each other makeovers!" Sydney exclaimed as she pushed Alice away from her.

"That sounds painful," I said.

"It's just makeup," Ginger countered.

"Stupid, painful, murderous makeup," I argued. "But if that's what you wanna do, I'll just go to bed."

"You can't go to bed *now*!" Sydney protested.

"Goodnight!" I rolled my eyes, laid down in my hammock, and fell asleep.

"Seriously, what teenager falls asleep at *nine* at a sleepover?" Sydney asked herself.

A Night of Doubts and Mysteries

Sydney's big night had come. Everyone was almost ready to leave for the palace, but Sydney was worrying so much that I began to hope we would never actually go to the ball.

"How bad does my makeup look?" Sydney asked me again.

"For the last time, Sydney, you look great," I urged.

"Does this dress make me look like a dork?" Sydney asked.

"No, but it's not like we have to actually go to the ball," I stalled.

"My shoulders aren't even," Sydney complained as she popped her back.

"No one cares about your shoulders," I countered.

"It's just not fair," Sydney sighed. "You're gorgeous and you already have a boy to love you and everything about you is perfect. And then you have me... some dork who isn't social at all, can't make a decision to save my life, and doesn't have many friends."

"Sydney, listen to me," I said. "You look beautiful, you're smart, you're funny, and you're brave... brave enough to go out there and have the night of your life."

"Okay, then," Sydney said, as she nodded. We soon left the harbor and made our way to the ball.

When we arrived, Michael greeted us at the entrance. He was dressed nicely, and had grey eyes and light brown hair. He was definitely short for his age, but something about him seemed strangely familiar, as though in his eyes laid a cruel but vague memory.

"Welcome to Kensington Palace," he greeted us. "I'm Michael Evans. My father is in King William's royal council."

"Hi... I... I am Sy... Sydney... um... h-hi," Sydney sheepishly stuttered, with a grin and red cheeks.

"Greetings, Sydney," Michael said, as he kissed Sydney's hand.

"You're hot!" Alice exclaimed.

"Yeah, you're really hot," Ginger agreed.

"You... you ha... have nice eyes," Sydney said, with her own eyes vacant and set on Michael.

"You're very beautiful, Sydney," Michael said.

Sydney, in shock, almost fainted and fell into Michael's arms. When she finally managed to remember how to stand up, Michael led Sydney inside. But somehow, I was worried for the two of them. Nothing about the boy himself seemed cruel, he just reminded me of something... or perhaps *someone*.

"Ryker, does that kid look familiar to you?" I asked.

"Maybe a little," he replied. "Why?"

"I don't know," I sighed. "There's just something about him... I can't place it, he just makes me feel uneasy."

"You're probably just nervous because you're in the palace and Sydney has a boyfriend now. Plus, Michael wouldn't hurt a fly. I don't think he physically can."

"Yeah, you're right," I said. "Did he have a ribbon in his hair?"

"Yep."

"Wow, what a dork! Sydney deserves better," I giggled. "Hey, we should spend the whole night making fun of Michael, to ease the pain of wearing this dress!"

"Or we could dance," Ryker suggested.

"No, never," I argued. Just the thought of dancing made me sick.

"Why, because you can't dance in heels?"

"Well..." I lifted my dress just enough to where Ryker could see the black tip of the pirate boots under my dress. I looked up at him and blushed.

"That makes sense," Ryker nodded. "But if you can fight sharks and run from volcanoes in those shoes, surely you can dance."

"Oh, Ryker, please, no," I begged. "I couldn't dance to save my life."

"Come on, you said you'd do anything for me," Ryker urged.

"Dancing doesn't count," I grumbled.

"Just for five minutes," Ryker pleaded.

"No," I moaned. I looked at Ryker, who was still smiling anxiously at me. He had won me over. I rolled my eyes. "Fine."

"Great, come on!" Ryker happily grabbed my hand and dragged me into the ballroom. The room was absolutely stunning. The ceiling was a high dome covered in murals. The walls were just as beautiful, adorned with flowers and paintings of kings and queens, sometimes opening into hallways. There were pillars draped in gold all around the place. On the opposite side of the room sat the king and queen. They were the most intimidating people I had ever seen... haughty, self-centered royals.

Ryker and I began to dance. Of course, I kept stepping on his feet, but Ryker didn't seem to mind. However, I couldn't stop looking at Sydney and Michael. I honestly was afraid for Sydney. Michael seemed completely harmless, but Sydney was my best friend and I had to look out for her.

The two of them were dancing together, each one seeming happy and content. They looked at each other as if the whole world had suddenly become perfect. I knew that feeling. Suddenly, Michael began to speak, but I couldn't make out what he was saying.

"So what made you leave that school?" Michael asked.

"It's not important," Sydney mumbled.

"Were you still being bullied?" Michael inquired.

"You know, you didn't have to barge in and yell at everyone that day. I would've been fine."

"No, nothing about that was 'fine'," Michael argued. "And I still don't think 'four eyes' is a suitable name for a girl as lovely as you."

"But I had eyeglasses; two real eyes and two glass ones," Sydney said.

"They were making fun of you, and you know it," Michael shook his head. "And I don't understand why the headmistress did nothing about it, considering the school belonged to her."

"Headmistress Evans was doing her job perfectly. Nothing needed to be done about me."

"Then why did you leave?"

"Michael, I was already alone, my leaving didn't make a difference to me or anyone else." Sydney looked down, trying to hide her tears.

"Then, let me promise you something," Michael lifted Sydney's chin. "As long as there is breath in my lungs, I will always be there for you and I will always love you. I'll never let you feel alone."

"Oh... thanks," Sydney whispered as she wiped her tears.

Michael looked into the crowd and motioned for someone to come over. A man and woman came, and Michael introduced Sydney to them.

"Sydney, meet my parents," he said. "This is my mother, Diane Evans, and my father, Sir Phillip Evans."

Sydney shook Sir Phillip's hand, but when she went to shake Diane's hand, Diane awkwardly jerked it away and put out her other hand.

"What's up with her?" I thought. "Why did she jerk her right hand away? She probably doesn't even have a right hand. Belle, you know that's not true. She's just left-handed, that's all. But that whole family really does look like a bunch of hoity-toity, stuck-up pigs. Well, then again, Michael's not so bad. Of course, any boy who wears tights and a hair ribbon is just strange. But he seems okay for Sydney, at least. But seriously, what, on Earth, does she see in him?"

"Belle, stop spying on Sydney and Michael," Ryker said.

"But they're just so… weird," I scoffed.

"No, they're just not like you," Ryker argued.

"His mother only has one hand," I said.

"Belle, that is the exact definition of paranoid," Ryker countered.

"And they are the exact definition of weird."

"They're fine, stop judging them."

"Michael is literally wearing tights, the child needs therapy."

"Did you say therapy?" Sawyer asked, startling me.

"Don't even think about it," Ryker grunted.

"Go ahead, make fun of the weirdo. See if I care." I motioned for Sawyer to leave.

Sawyer walked over to Sydney and Michael as Ginger and Alice followed him.

"Excuse me, are you mentally ill?" Sawyer tugged Michael's jacket.

"Why would I be mentally ill?" Michael asked.

"I don't know, Belle just said you needed therapy," Sawyer replied.

"You're hot!" Ginger exclaimed.

"You know," Alice hinted, "if things between you and Sydney don't work out…"

"They most certainly will," Michael assured her.

"Go away," Sydney whined.

"That's no way to talk to a man!" Sawyer scolded.

"I wasn't talking to a man, I was talking to you," Sydney retorted.

"I am a man!" Sawyer informed her. "And I also have one chest hair!"

"Nobody asked, doofus," Alice rolled her eyes. "And I'll have you know that if you don't stop bragging about your stupid chest hair, I'll chop it off in your sleep!"

"No, don't hurt my precious chest hair!" Sawyer pleaded.

"If you say the words 'chest hair' one more time, I am going to slap that stupid little grin right off of your face!" Alice threatened.

"Chest hair!" Sawyer yelled.

"Alright, that's it!" Alice screamed as she tried to slap Sawyer, but Ginger quickly grabbed her arm.

"Alice, can't this wait until the king and queen aren't staring at us? You're gonna get us in trouble!" Ginger begged.

"Fine, then, I'll wait," Alice resolved.

Away from all of this, Ryker and I continued to dance, but I couldn't help but notice the fact that Diane kept staring at me and was whispering something about it to her husband. I assumed she was judging me. After all, I was anything but a lady.

To make matters worse, my bun was killing me. It was so tight I felt as though it would tear my face off, and it was giving me a terrible headache.

"This stupid bun is making my head hurt," I groaned.

"Then take it down," Ryker suggested.

"I can't. It's too tight," I complained.

"Turn around. I'll get it for you," Ryker said. I turned around and after struggling for a few minutes Ryker took my hair down. Two and a half feet of hair fell below my waist and I turned back around. Ryker looked at me, stunned.

"What?" I asked.

"You're just... you... you're... gorgeous," Ryker stammered.

"You think so?"

"Yeah, of course. I mean, you'd pass for a lady, if I didn't know any better."

"Look, I know that's just you saying I'm pretty, but you know I hate being called... "

"No, you are," Ryker reassured me. I looked past him and saw Diane look at me, put her hand over her mouth in shock, and begin to make her way toward us.

When she reached us, she asked, "Young lady, what is your name?"

"Belle Smith," I answered. "Don't call me a lady."

She awkwardly said, "Yes, thank you." Then, she walked away.

"What was that for?" I asked.

"I don't know," Ryker returned.

"Wow, you're so helpful," I said sarcastically. "I have got to get out of this mad house. That lady is still staring at me."

"She probably has a friend that looks like you," Ryker guessed.

"I still think she's weird."

"Just forget about it," Ryker pleaded.

"Fine, whatever," I grunted. I figured if I couldn't obsess over Diane, I could obsess over Michael and Sydney. I couldn't help it. I was worried about Sydney and how this would all turn out, and I was bored out of my mind. So, I looked over at the couple. They were talking and dancing happily until something very abrupt and unexpected happened. They stopped dancing and Michael leaned closer to Sydney. Sydney's hands began to tremble. And suddenly, Michael kissed her. Sydney stood in shock, shaking even more. Then, to my surprise, she backed away from him and ran into the hallway.

"I'll be right back," I told Ryker.

"What? Why?"

"Sydney's upset."

"No one cares about Sydney," Ryker objected.

"I do," I argued. I ran into the hallway and found Sydney sitting against a wall in tears.

"So… Michael kissed you… exciting!" I started.

"No, that's not exciting," Sydney denied. "That's the reason I'm upset."

"But why would that make you upset?" I sat down next to her.

Sydney sighed. "When Michael kissed me, the whole world felt perfect. It felt as though I was living in a fairy tale. Then I realized I was. That moment was just *too* perfect. It was *too* good to be true. Listen, Michael's not like Ryker. He's not running away from anything. Michael loves it here. But I don't belong here. I don't fit in. And being with Michael will never work because he can't leave and I can't stay. I don't know why I even tried. There's just no one out there for me."

"But if he loves you, he'll come with you, won't he?"

"I don't even know what love is, much less *true* love," Sydney sniffled.

"Well, Sydney, from what I know, love is always caring for someone and never giving up on them. Love is holding someone accountable, but also forgiving. It's being able to trust someone, and them being able to trust you. It's not jealous, selfish, proud, or unkind in any way. It's keeping your promises. It's always being there for someone when they need you. And it's one of the most important things you could ever give.

"Now *true* love, that's another story. True love, as I would put it, is when there's this one person in your life that you will genuinely love forever. It's a selfless bond that even death, itself, can't break. And you can't stop loving this person, because you honestly don't know how, even if you think you hate them. It doesn't matter how many times they break your heart, you still pursue them. And you're willing to give anything and everything for them, even your very life. You're there when they need you, and you never forsake them. Where they go in life, you follow. And they do the same for you."

"But he kissed me," Sydney sobbed. "Listen, you don't understand. I don't know how to respond to someone falling in love with me, or kissing me. And now I wish Michael had never even met me."

"But don't you love him?" I inquired.

"Yes, I would do anything for him. I would stay here and just put up with that stupid school, I truly would, but I don't fit in here. I fit in on the *Pegasus*."

"Then take the idiot with you," I suggested. "But only if he loses the tights and ponytail, okay?"

"Michael's not just gonna run away from his home."

"But he'll run away with you."

Sydney looked at me and smiled, and I gave her a hug. But we were both startled when we heard a terrible scream and a loud shout. "There's been a robbery in the palace!"

We rushed into the ballroom, only to find everyone in tumult and chaos, and Diane lying unconscious on the floor.

Disaster in Kensington Palace

Sydney and I rushed toward Diane. Michael and his father worriedly came, too. Diane's face was pale; she looked like she'd seen a ghost... or worse. She looked absolutely traumatized, as though shock and fear had overtaken her.

"Mother!" Michael cried. "Mother, wake up! Please!"

"She's sick, Son, she won't be waking up for a while," Sir Phillip said gruffly.

"No, no she's not sick," I corrected, pushing through the crowd. "It's trauma. She's shocked."

"Oh please, she's not traumatized. She's sick," Phillip denied.

"Sir, I've seen that look on her face. I know that look. She…"

"I will not listen to a pirate such as you, you imbecile!" the man snapped.

"Father, she's been invited here, she won't hurt anyone," Michael reassured.

"As long as I am living, she is not welcome here. She is no different than a stupid, murderous, wretched pirate!" Phillip screamed.

"No, you don't understand," I pleaded. "I'm not…"

"Shut up!" He yelled as he slapped me across the face. My first reaction was to punch him back, and I did. He almost tried to fight me, when a voice stopped him.

"I saw him!" Diane wailed. "I saw him!"

"Who, darling? Who did you see?" Her husband rushed to her.

"*Clark Teach*," Diane said faintly. Just the sound of his name made me shudder. His name was known all around the palace, but Diane seemed to know a little more than the others. But how? She couldn't have known Clark. That would have been impossible.

"What is going on?" King William came to the situation, oblivious to this tragic event.

"The palace has been robbed," a guard informed him, as he handed him a crinkled envelope. "This was found where the jewels used to be."

"*To Belle Smith, from Dylan Crow. Only read this if you can handle the truth*," the king read.

"That's me," I said. "I'm Belle Smith."

King William handed over the envelope. I went into another room and opened it. The paper was worn and the handwriting was messy. I read:

Dear Belle,

Soon after you ran away, the crew member told me some important stuff about your past. I thought it was about time you also knew.

It all started on the Pegasus. You see, your father, Jacob Smith, was the captain, and your mother, Lilly, was his first mate. They were both good and honest people, a lot like you, with a good crew... well, except for Clark Teach.

Clark, at one point, had a wife. I don't know what idiot would marry him, but that's not the point. She was a kind woman, but very naïve. In January of 1680, she gave birth to twins. However, one was born ill and very small. This made Clark furious. He even tried to kill his wife and her baby. She escaped with the child and only one hand. The other child was raised to be as evil as Clark himself and was sent away to form his own crew, very young.

All this time, Clark had been planning a mutiny. And, in November of 1682, I am sorry to tell you that he murdered both of your parents. They didn't drown, that's just what Clark wanted you to think. Greed took over his heart, and he's only gotten worse. He tried to kill you, but then he realized that he could use you. I had secretly been in his wife's care for a while, but I felt sorry for you and wanted to help you, even though I was only four at the time. Actually, Clark's wife was the one who taught me how to read, even when she was in hiding. That way, I could teach you. Soon after, Clark found a new ship, the Cobra, and abandoned the Pegasus. That is when his wife escaped, but Clark caught the two of us.

That is the reason I told you to leave this wretched place when I did. I knew where we were at the time. I knew there was an abandoned ship nearby, I just didn't know the story behind it yet. It's your inheritance, Belle. It was meant for you. I also broke into the palace with Clark and his terrible crew to tell you this and ask for help. Please, whoever the king sends, tell them that we will be in Crossbone Cove, on the northwest side of Sweden. And send someone for me. Clark has treated me like dirt my whole life. He's turned me into another person. I know I've never been innocent, but working for Clark is… it's so bad I don't even know how to say it. I don't know how much longer I can live like this… or live at all.

Sincerely,
Dylan Crow

I didn't know what to think of this. I began to cry, but not tears of grief. I had already grieved over my parents. I already knew they were dead. What I had never known was that there was someone to blame for their deaths. I wasn't sad now, I was angry. I had never been so angry because there was never anyone to blame. But now, it was different. In a blind rage, I screamed as I picked up an oil lamp and threw it across the room. I didn't know why I had done so, but I did know one thing. I wanted revenge. I longed for it more than anything in the world.

At that moment, Ryker came rushing into the room. He found me there, crying against the wall.

"Belle?" he asked. "Belle, what happened?"

"Go away," I sobbed.

"I'm not leaving until you tell me," Ryker objected.

"Please, just go," I begged.

"I'm just trying to help," Ryker pleaded. "What is going on?"

"He murdered my parents," I stammered after a while.

"Who?"

"Clark, you idiot!" I screamed angrily.

"Belle, you don't have to get mad at me," Ryker countered. "I'm only trying to help."

"Well, you're not helping, so just leave me alone!" I cried.

"No! I'm not leaving!" Ryker yelled.

"You just wouldn't understand. You would never understand," I said dismally.

"I don't care about whether or not I understand," Ryker argued. "I care about *you*."

"Alright then," I started. "You wanna know what's wrong? Maybe it hasn't occurred to you that my parents were *murdered!* All my life, I've been an orphan, Ryker. I've never had much, and I grew up having to provide for myself and keep myself alive. I had Dylan, but he was barely even alive himself. I have always wanted parents, and I always just assumed there was nothing anyone could do about their deaths. I was never angry because there was no one to be angry at. But apparently, all of my life I've been believing a lie! Clark took my parents from me, and abused me for ten years! He turned an innocent girl's childhood into a living nightmare! I always knew he was evil but I never realized just how much. And the results fell on my family! My parents didn't deserve to die! *He* did, and he always will! I hate him! You know what, why don't I just kill him? That'll make things right. Then I can put to death my pain, along with the evil man who caused it!

That's what I'll do. That'll fix everything. I'll just kill him! I'll kill him!"

"Belle!" Ryker stopped me. "Revenge won't bring your parents back. And it won't make things better. And if you're so mad at Clark for killing your parents, you're just as bad, if you kill him."

I stared at Ryker in shock at what I had been saying. But he was right. I had gone completely insane. I suddenly began to cry even more, feeling terrible for what I had just said. Ryker wrapped his arms around me, trying to do whatever he could to comfort me.

"It's okay, calm down." Ryker wiped my tears. "I'm right here. I'll do whatever you need."

"There's nothing you can do. Clark took everything from me. I have nothing," I sobbed.

"You have me," Ryker said. "And I promise I will always be with you. I won't let anyone take me from you."

"Please don't leave me," I begged. "I need you. You're the only one I have left."

"Belle, you know I could never leave you. I love you."

"I love you, too," I said in tears.

"You're gonna be okay," Ryker assured me. "You're strong, you'll be just fine. I know your life is tough, but you're tougher. And I'm right here for you."

Suddenly, a noble flung the door open and worriedly exclaimed, "Alright, children, time's up! How could you be kissing at a time like this? Out! Shoo! Begone!"

Ryker and I hurried away into the ballroom, which was in chaos.

"Yes, it was Clark Teach! I saw him! I promise I saw him!" Diane pleaded with the king.

"I'm sorry, Mrs. Evans, but we can't believe you. You have no proof. You could be delusional, as far as we know," King William debated.

"I have proof," I broke in, as I handed the letter to the king.

He examined the letter and said, "I see, but how do we know it wasn't you? How can we believe this letter is true?"

"Please, sir, Belle is the most trustworthy girl I know," Ryker informed him. "She would never rob you, nor lie to you."

"Show me the letter," Diane demanded. The king passed her the letter and she read it carefully. After a minute, she clarified, "The letter is fully true. I know things about this man. The writer is correct."

"And how would you know?" King William inquired. "Have you met this man?"

"No! No!" Diane shrieked. "I just know many things about him."

"She did see him, honestly," Michael assured the king.

"Well, if Clark Teach has robbed the castle, what are we supposed to do about it?" King William asked.

"We will send our navy to find him and arrest him, and bring back the items he has stolen," his advisor suggested.

"No!" the king fumed. "I will not allow you to bring that evil man into my city. He'll just break out of prison and destroy all of England!"

"And I will not send my fleet in pursuit of Clark! We'll all be dead the moment we see him!" the navy's captain objected.

"But I have a friend, he's trapped there," I cried, with no one's permission. "If you don't save him, he'll die!"

"I will not allow a girl, much less a pirate, to order me around!" King William yelled. "You shouldn't even be here!"

"I invited her, along with Sydney," Michael admitted.

"They're pirates, you fool!" King William shouted.

"Please, sir, I beg of you, please send someone to help him," I screamed.

"No!" the king shrieked.

"But he'll die!" I sobbed.

"Well, some people just have to die!" the king thundered. "And it's not as if I would even care what you would have to say to me! Not only are you both a child and a girl, but you are a pirate!"

"Why can't you just take someone else's words into consideration, for once in your life?" Ryker yelled. "I don't care what you think. Stop shaming my girlfriend!"

"Shut up!" King William shouted.

"Do you have a navy of cowards, or are you gonna go after Clark?" Ryker asked.

"I will never go after Clark!"

"I will," I said abruptly. "It has to be done. You may be too afraid, but I'm not. We'll leave tomorrow. I may pick up some of your stupid jewels if I have the time."

"Belle, no," Ryker whispered. "You can't..."

"I will also go," Michael offered. I rolled my eyes.

Diane's eyes suddenly filled with terror. "No, darling. You will not..."

"I must, Mother," Michael interrupted. "I couldn't bear to let Sydney leave without me. I love her to the ends of the earth. I wouldn't exchange her safety for anything in the world. And I must be loyal to my king."

"Sydney will be fine. You are the one that needs safety," Diane pleaded.

"I don't care about my safety," Michael argued.

"Well, I do, and I won't let you go," Diane objected.

"Mother," Michael begged.

"No! You will stay here and that's final!" Diane yelled.

Michael looked at me with pleading eyes.

"I'm sorry," I started. "You just... you just don't have what it takes."

"Why not?" Michael asked. "What makes you any different than me?"

"Our mothers weren't there to hold us back," I answered. I turned around and left Kensington Palace with the rest of the Stowaways.

A New Voyage

I opened my eyes and blinked, in my hammock. Morning had come. That wretched, dreadful night was over. I soon remembered my proclamation to rescue Dylan and bring back the king's stolen riches. I knew it seemed outlandish, but it had to be done. It was my responsibility. It was time. If no one else was going to confront Clark, I would. If no one other ship was going to sail to Crossbone Cove, the *Pegasus* would.

I stood up from my hammock, got dressed, and went into the hold of the ship. Ryker was already there, looking into different crates and barrels.

"How long have you been down here?" I asked.

"A while," he answered. "I was just checking to see if we had everything we needed."

"Do we?" I rummaged through a barrel of maps and pulled one out.

"Yeah, and I went ahead and put the tea where Sawyer can't reach it. Is something wrong?"

"No," I replied, "but I just realized that we have to go through the North Sea to get to Sweden."

"What's so bad about that?"

"Ryker, it's November. It's cold. It'll be even colder on the North Sea."

"Well, you know, we don't have to go, if you're not up for it," Ryker suggested.

"No, Ryker," I argued. "I have to go. Dylan kept me alive for ten years, I can't let him die now."

"Yeah... right." Ryker hesitated.

"You okay?"

"Yeah... yeah, I'm fine," Ryker denied.

"No, you're not fine. You're being weird. Just tell me. I won't be upset," I urged.

"No, I shouldn't tell you. I don't even know if it's true."

"Ryker, please, you know I love you and you know I care about what you have to say. Just tell me. I'll listen," I begged.

"I just... I can't lose you," Ryker admitted.

"To Clark?"

"Well, yes, and maybe..."

"No, you don't think I'm in love with *Dylan*, do you?" I gasped.

"No! No, I would never think that. I know I can trust you. It's not you, it's me."

"What do you mean?"

"Well, you know I can't measure up to him. He's done everything for you. I haven't really done much of anything," Ryker sighed.

"But you're perfect for me. I need you. And believe me, you are more than enough for me. Dylan may have saved my life, but he could never take your place in my heart. You've done so much for me, Ryker. And I won't allow you to think otherwise. You're more amazing than I could even imagine. Trust me, I will always love you. Plus, Dylan's practically my brother."

"I love you, too... always," Ryker promised. He took my hands and kissed me.

Suddenly, Sydney walked in and whined, "I wanna do that with Michael!"

"But when Michael kissed you, you started crying," I argued.

"I don't care!" Sydney groaned. "I miss Michael."

"Yeah, Belle, go get Michael," Ryker pleaded.

"Why do you care?" I asked.

"Because Sawyer's the only other boy in the crew, and he's getting dumber every day," Ryker answered.

"Hey, Belle, is my medallion necklace in that barrel?" Sydney asked.

"Let me see." I opened the barrel and suddenly jumped back and screamed.

"Rat! Rat! There's a rat!" I shrieked.

"Let me see!" Sydney exclaimed. She peeked inside the barrel, *reached in*, and pulled out the strange-looking creature.

"Oh, it's not a rat at all! This is a ferret! Isn't he adorable?" she mused.

"No, he's ugly," Ryker countered.

"Not as ugly as you," Sydney retorted.

"Oh, please. That thing's gonna make the Black Plague happen all over again," Ryker objected.

"No, he's not," Sydney said sweetly, just before *kissing* the ferret's loathsome little cheek.

"Maybe your necklace is in here," I said, as I opened another barrel. "Oh, look! Another rat!"

Ryker looked inside the barrel. "Michael? Hey... he's not a rat!"

"Michael! Michael! How... how did you get here?" Sydney exclaimed.

"I snuck out last night so that I could be with you," Michael admitted. I rolled my eyes.

"But why, on Earth, would you want to leave London?" Sydney asked.

"I love you," Michael answered, as he kissed Sydney's cheek.

"I... well... I mean..." Sydney stuttered.

"Well, we don't need two new crew members; the rat has to go," Ryker said.

"Bye, bye, Michael!" I exclaimed.

"No! No! I need a roommate that doesn't drive me insane!" Ryker objected.

"And I need a boyfriend!" Sydney added.

"Fine, then we'll lose the other rat," I ordered.

"No! Not Gerald Templeton!" Sydney screamed.

"You *named* him?" I shrieked.

"Jerry for short!" Sydney replied.

"Get rid of him!" I demanded.

"Oh, come on, Belle," Sydney pleaded. "You can't turn someone down just because of how they look. Remember what happened to Alice?"

"Alice is a human. Jerry's a rat," I countered.

"Well, he still has feelings," Sydney said.

"Me too. Bad feelings about this rat," I said.

"But ferrets are smart! He can steal back the jewels!" Sydney argued.

"Yeah, right," I scoffed.

"No, really! It's true!"

"What gives you a say, anyway?" Michael asked.

"I'm the captain."

"A girl captain! Who would have thought of such a thing?" Michael laughed.

Ryker and I looked judgingly at Michael.

"You know what? Fine! Fine! Keep the rat! I don't care anymore!" I yelled.

"Did you hear that, Jerry? You get to be a Stowaway! Yay!" Sydney exclaimed.

"And enough with the baby talk, already!" I begged. Sydney and Michael were about to walk away, when I said, "Michael, get back here!"

"Why?" he asked.

"I need to tell you our many rules. Plus, you're already breaking them. Come on," I replied.

"One moment, Sydney," Michael said, turning towards me.

"Does any of this involve me?" Ryker asked.

"No," I answered. Ryker left and I began to speak. "Alright, here we go. Tights are not permitted under any circumstance. I think they're stupid, dorky, and unnecessary. Boys can't wear hair ribbons. That's also dorky. No fancy suits, no gowns, no Pilgrim dresses."

"Well, then, what am I supposed to wear?" Michael retorted.

"Not *that*," I said, pointing to Michael's clothing. "Anyway… if you're gonna fire a gun, do it outside. Don't blow a hole in the ship and don't shoot anyone. Don't make Alice mad. She might beat you up, if you do. Don't make Sydney mad, either. She's a high-maintenance nervous wreck when she's mad. Then, she starts trying to walk through doors *before* she opens them, and then she starts yelling at people for no reason. Yes, this happens all the time.

"Also, don't make me mad. I have a sword and I'm not afraid to use it. As for Ginger, she doesn't get mad. Like, ever. And don't take any advice from Sawyer. Don't make any bargains with Sawyer. And please, please don't give Sawyer any sugar. You know what, just don't associate with Sawyer at all, okay? He's a mad genius, but also a doofus, at the same time. Don't question my authority. Just do yourself a favor and listen to me. Last but not least, if a fight breaks out, don't kill each other. Don't break any bones. You can do that some other time."

"Are you done?" Michael pleaded.

"Yes, but one more thing," I said. "Sydney is my best friend. Now that you're her boyfriend, you're responsible for her. I expect you to love and care for her. And if you break her heart, I'll break your neck. Understand?"

"Don't worry. I'll always love Sydney."

"Alright then. You're part of the crew."

Michael thanked me and went to look for Sydney. I decided to try and find Ginger. Of all of us, she would need the most help, for sure. I found her in her room, still in her nightgown.

"Hey, Ginger!" I greeted her.

"Oh, good morning," she returned. "Do you need me?"

"Yeah, come on," I said. "We need to find you something to wear."

"Oh, don't worry," Ginger replied. "I brought plenty of dresses."

"Sorry, but you can't really wear those when you're a pirate," I objected.

"Oh." Ginger followed me into a storage room, where some old clothes were laying around.

I looked around and found a small jacket, a white shirt, and a skirt made of black and red cloth. I tossed them to her and told her to try them on while I finished preparations for our departure. I went onto the deck to hoist the sails. I went around to let everyone know we were leaving. Finally, Ryker lifted the anchor. A new voyage had just begun in pursuit of the infamous Captain Clark Teach.

"Belle! Help!" Alice screamed, as she ran onto the deck. "I woke up and Ginger was gone! I think I scared her away!"

"You probably did," Ryker muttered.

"Ginger's in the storage hold," I told Alice. "She's finding an outfit."

"How do I look?" Ginger emerged from below deck.

"Great!" I exclaimed. Then, I called for Michael.

"You wanted to see me?" he asked. "What's wrong?"

"Your dorky hair," I answered. "Now, hold still."

"Why? What are you going to do?" Michael asked anxiously.

"I'm going to cut your hair," I replied. I drew my sword to his neck.

"You're going to cut my head off!" Michael squealed.

"No, I'm going to cut your hair off," I corrected him.

"No! Stop! Don't cut my beautiful hair!" Michael whined.

"Oh, please, your hair is anything but beautiful," I scoffed as I cut his hair in one slice. Now, it was just short enough to keep away from that stupid little ribbon, which I decided to throw into the ocean.

"There," I concluded. "*Now* you're a Stowaway."

Unlocking the Past

It was midnight. I couldn't sleep, and I couldn't stop thinking about my parents. What were they like? What did they do with their crew? What did they look like? The fact that I didn't even know broke my heart. I figured I wouldn't be able to sleep, if I didn't at least try to get up and find something.

I stood up, opened my desk drawer, and pulled out a key. I never knew what it was used for, but I figured it had something to do with my parents. I grabbed a lamp and went to the back of the ship below deck. I rummaged through all of the barrels and chests and treasures we had, until I came upon one mysterious-looking chest. The name 'Smith' was engraved into the wood. I pushed the key into the lock and turned it. The chest opened!

Inside was a portrait of my parents, Jacob and Lilly Smith. My mother looked just like me. She had bright green eyes, freckles, and straight blonde hair that she wore down to her waist. She wore a white blouse with a leather corset over it, large hoop earrings, and a compass around her neck. My father had eyes as blue as the sea. His light brown hair was pulled back and tucked under his hat. He held a spyglass and a map.

I began to cry. I had never known what my parents had looked like. This was like a glimpse into the past, into a world I had never come to know. I stroked my hand down the portrait, as though I could just reach out and touch them. But I couldn't. They were gone from this world. If I called out to them, they'd never answer. If I told them about my problems, they'd never know. Even if they were looking down at me from Heaven, it just wasn't the same.

Continuing to look through the chest, I found my mother's compass, which I put around my neck, my father's spyglass and hat, and my mother's diary. I flipped through the old, tattered pages. Wanting to know more, I took the diary back to my room, sat down at my desk, and decided to read the first entry.

Lilly Wilson, 1675

After almost being murdered, then being saved, and then running away with a band of pirates, I figured it was about time to keep a diary. It only seemed suitable to record my voyages.

But let me tell you how I came to be on the Pegasus. It started in my childhood. I lived in Salem. I was a Puritan... or at least I was supposed to be. I knew and loved God with my whole heart, but I could never please and obey my parents the way they wanted me to. Everyone looked down upon me, telling me that I didn't behave properly, didn't dress suitably, and wasn't a good enough Puritan.

Just yesterday, my mother rebuked my outfit so much that I couldn't help but tell her that God didn't care how I dressed at all. Then, the community concluded that I was a disgrace to the Wilson family and a witch. How absurd! I am only human, I'm fifteen years old, and I'm no witch. I had no trial and I had no rights whatsoever. This morning they even attempted to hang me! My hands were tied and a rope had been put around my neck. I hopelessly prayed for a miracle and braced myself for my death.

Then, the strangest thing happened. A ship began to pull into our harbor. It had white sails and a Pegasus carved into the bow.

Suddenly, a crew of pirates emerged from the ship and made their way into the village! Everyone was panicking and there was chaos everywhere. And then the captain, a young, handsome man with bright blue eyes and light brown hair, approached me. He said, "Hello, fair lady," to me and cut the ropes around me. He took my hand and led me to the ship. I decided to run away with him. I didn't care if he was a pirate. At least he accepted me.

I looked up in shock. Had my mother really been a *Puritan*? Of all people, how could my mother have been one of those? It made sense that she didn't belong. She couldn't have. She belonged with my father.

I was now very curious about my mother, so I flipped through the pages, skipping a few at a time, and kept on reading.

Lilly Wilson, 1676

I know I've been a pirate for a while now, but I'm beginning to feel strange about Jacob. Whenever he speaks to me, I blush. Whenever he takes my hand, I tremble. When I look into his eyes, I feel as though I can never leave him. Am I falling in love? What's more, has he always loved me? Wait… what am I saying? That's impossible. Well, I guess it's good no one will ever read this.

Lilly Wilson, 1676

Jacob kissed me. I didn't know what to do when he did. All I knew was that someone finally loves me. And I love him. I want to be with him forever. It's for certain now; we were destined to be together.

Lilly Smith, 1678

Last night was the most magical night of my life. Jacob and I were just talking as normal, but something felt different. Then, all of a sudden, he knelt down and pulled a ring out from his pocket. It was beautiful, covered in gold, sapphires, and diamonds. And at that moment, Jacob asked me for my hand in marriage. I immediately said "yes". We were married right away. I am now proud to be both a Smith, and the happiest woman alive.

Lilly Smith, 1679

We've just recruited two new crewmates: Clark Teach and his wife. However, this Clark makes me very nervous. He always speaks with a sly voice, and there's always anger behind his eyes. He'll get upset so easily and will begin to fight when he doesn't get what he wants. He uses anyone he can to please himself. If he can't use someone, he then hates them. It's no wonder why his wife is so timorous. She won't speak at all to anyone. Most of us don't even know her name or anything about her. But I'm worried about Clark. It's obvious he's jealous of Jacob's position. He seems the type of man who would start a murderous rebellion, but that's just what I think.

Lilly Smith, 1680

A tragic thing has happened. Last night, Clark's wife finally had her twins. I didn't know what was going on, but I could hear Clark raging at her, and she was screaming in terror. This morning, she was gone. She had vanished, along with one of the boys. I thought Clark was behind this, so I snuck into his room. I searched for a sign, or a clue of some sort. When I opened one of his drawers, I was baffled at what I saw: a hand and a bloodstained knife. I immediately knew that something was terribly wrong.

I soon found her hiding in the very back of the cargo hold. She was pale and her hair was a mess. She told me that because one of her children was born with an illness that made him smaller than the other, Clark was displeased. He told her that the child was a useless piece of garbage that should be done away with. He then tried to murder his wife and child, leaving her only one choice: to run away and hide with her son. I offered to take care of her since she could not show her face on the Pegasus anymore. I knew I couldn't tell Jacob. If I did, Clark would be furious.

Lilly Smith, 1682

A few hours ago I heard a gunshot. I came out onto the deck to see what had happened, and my eyes filled with tears when I found Jacob lying helpless in his own blood. He said that Clark had shot him, wanting to be captain. Jacob kissed me one last time. And with his last breath, he said he would always love me. I told him that I would always love him, too, but he was gone.

But if Clark murdered Jacob for his position, that means I'm next. I can't hide, because the Pegasus needs a captain. I can't stay, because I have to be alive to raise Belle. I love my crew, but Belle comes first. I'll hide with Diane and I can escape with her. If I die, she can take care of Belle. If she dies or runs away, Belle will just have to be raised by Dylan, the little boy who's sometimes with Diane. I can't trust her with anyone else. Everyone in our crew is either on Clark's side or will be once he takes over. I just wish I had told Jacob sooner. Then, none of this would have ever happened. Jacob didn't deserve to die, and Belle doesn't deserve to live in hiding. After all, she just turned two, a month ago. If only I could have...

The passage stopped mid-sentence. The writing had been stained red with blood. All of the pages after that were empty. My mother had been slaughtered while writing her very last journal entry.

The Last Compass

Unfortunately, morning came sooner than I wanted it to. I woke up to Sydney screaming, "Gerald Templeton, you get back here right this instant! Jerry! Jerry, come back! No, not Belle's room!"

I reluctantly lifted my head to find that Jerry had slid under my bedroom door. I knelt down and picked him up.

"What's your problem, anyway?" I asked him, not as if he would answer.

"*Squawk!* I don't have any problems, unlike you," Donna screeched. "I mean, what girl gets mad at her boyfriend for sacrificing his life? I'm just a little concerned…"

"I wasn't talking to you," I interrupted.

"Then who were you talking to?" Donna inquired.

"No one," I mumbled.

"*Squawk!* Were you talking to the rat? You really need therapy, Belle."

"He's not a rat! Let me in!" Sydney yelled, banging on the door.

"He looks like a rat to me!" Donna screeched.

"He's a ferret, mind you! He's a very exotic pet!" Sydney clarified.

"Exotic?" Donna exclaimed.

"Give me back my pet!" Sydney demanded.

"One moment, Sydney," I said, as I quickly got dressed.

"Ten more seconds!" Sydney called.

"Give me a minute, I'm almost out," I said.

"What's going on?" I heard Michael ask.

"Belle is holding Jerry captive!" Sydney cried. "Six... five..."

"Here." I opened the door and handed Jerry over to Sydney.

"Thanks, it took you long enough," Sydney said. "Hey, that's such a pretty necklace on you!"

"It's not a necklace. It's a compass," I said. "It was my mother's."

"Good morning!" Ginger exclaimed, as she pulled Alice onto the deck.

"Oh, Alice, you're up early," Sydney acknowledged.

"Eight o'clock isn't early," Ginger argued.

"It is for me," Alice whined. "I wanna go back to bed. I'm just a child!"

"Where's Ryker and Sawyer?" I asked.

"Sawyer's asleep. Ryker's drawing a mustache on Sawyer's face," Michael answered.

"Oh no," Alice said. "Sawyer's gonna use his fake mustache to flirt with me. I am so sick of that doofus."

"Are you, though? Are you really?" Sydney inquired.

"Yes," Alice assured her.

"Hey, guys," Ryker said, as he climbed onto the deck.

"Ryker, Sawyer's gonna try to flirt with me and it's all your fault!" Alice kicked Ryker in the shin.

"Well, I can't exactly say that I'm sorry," Ryker replied, pushing Alice away.

"Hey, Belle, can I see that necklace?" Sydney asked.

"Sure, and it's a compass," I answered, as I handed Sydney the necklace.

"Wait, Belle, you're wearing jewelry?" Ryker asked.

"No, for the last time, it's just my mother's old compass," I clarified.

"Does it still work?" Michael questioned.

"Yeah," Sydney said, as she gave the compass to Michael.

"Wow, this is quite a nice compass," Michael said. He began to twirl the chain around on his finger. It was making me nervous and I tried to stop him.

"If you drop that thing in the sea, I swear…"

And then my mother's compass flew off of Michael's finger and into the sea.

"Well, thanks a lot, Michael!" I rolled my eyes just before jumping into the sea. I could see the compass sinking just a few feet away from me, but as I reached for it, a swift current swept it away. I came up to breathe and then followed the current. I saw the compass again and swam down to get it.

As I swam, I noticed a shape off in the distance. It was blurry, but I assumed it was a shark. I knew that it would attack me if I made any noise or if it smelled blood, but I wasn't too afraid. My compass had fallen in between two rocks. When I tried to grab it, I cut my hand on a rock and squealed a little. I had a little more reason to be afraid now.

I quickly took my compass and swam away. I finally came up for air and tried not to look back at the shark. But I knew I wasn't fast enough. I looked back. The shark was coming. The shining compass had signaled it. I couldn't get away.

The shark came closer. Before it could strike me, I kicked its eye to fend it off. It didn't flinch. I struck its gills with my fist. It was hurt, but it decided to fight back. It burst out of the water and came down with a huge splash that knocked me back. The saltwater got into my eyes and my vision was blurred. I was now oblivious to the shark. I was blinded to it. It came around my back and bit my leg. It stung like a thousand knives and I screamed in pain, but I wouldn't let this go. If the shark fought back, then I would have to fight back, too. I swam towards the shark and punched its eye. I then climbed onto its back, grabbed its fin, and dug my foot into its gills. The shark jumped into the air, as I held on.

"Somebody get me a gun. I'm gonna shoot it," Ryker demanded.

"No! You'll just end up shooting Belle!" Sydney objected.

"Well, then, what do you want me to do?" Ryker yelled.

"Go swim over there and help her!" Sydney ordered.

"Sydney, I can't fight a shark with my bare hands," Ryker argued.

"Then take a sword," Sydney suggested.

"I can't swim and carry a sword."

"Well, then, what can you do?"

"I don't know!"

"Then figure it out!"

"Fine," Ryker concluded. "I'll go in a lifeboat. Then, I can take swords to fight with and bring Belle back without her having to swim."

"What do you want me to do?" Michael asked.

"Be less of an idiot next time," Ryker said. "No offense, buddy, but this is pretty much all your fault."

"Got it," Michael said.

Ryker jumped into a lifeboat with two swords. His plan was okay, but it was going to take him a while to get to me. So, I continued to fight the shark. It usually wasn't this difficult to do. Most of the time I would have a sword. Then again, most of the time I wouldn't be fighting a shark in the first place. I continued to clutch the fin on its back because I could no longer swim. Just when I thought things couldn't get any worse, the shark leaped into the air. I fell off of its back into the water. I struggled back up to the surface. I could hardly breathe now, much less fend off an angry shark.

Ryker, seeing there was no time left to spare, jumped out of the boat with two swords. He landed on the shark's back and dug the swords into both of its eyes. Ryker pulled the swords out and the shark swam away.

Ryker dropped the swords and took me back to the lifeboat. I closed my eyes and tried to catch my breath.

"Please tell me you got your compass," Ryker said after a while.

"Yeah... yeah, it's right... right here," I panted.

"I am going to kill Michael when we get back," Ryker said. "How are you doing?"

"I'm... I'm okay," I answered.

"I'm so sorry I didn't get there sooner. You almost died."

"Well, either way, you saved my life, so thanks a lot."

"Any time."

We finally came back to the *Pegasus* and Sydney helped us onto the ship.

"Oh my gosh!" she exclaimed. "Are you okay? That looks bad!"

"I'm fine," I replied. "I just can't walk."

"Then I'll carry you," Sydney proclaimed.

"Do yourself a favor and let me carry her," Ryker offered.

"Yes! Let Ryker carry me!" I agreed.

Just then, Sawyer and his dorky little mustache climbed onto the deck. He walked over to Alice, grabbed her hand, and said, "Hey, babe. Are you a booger? Cause I pick you."

"Get away from me, you creep!" Alice shrieked, as she punched Sawyer in the nose. I didn't even care at this point.

Donna, the Legendary Flag Guardian

A few days passed. I felt better and I was able to walk again. All morning Ryker and I had been navigating the *Pegasus* through the cold waters of the North Sea. I could do it alone, but Ryker made good company and was nice to be around. Sydney and Michael were ordered to clean the deck, which they hated doing. As for the younger kids, they just sat around below deck, bored out of their minds.

"I'm bored," Alice groaned. "Sawyer, can I take it out on you?"

"What do you mean?" Sawyer asked nervously.

"I need someone to punch!" Alice held up her fists.

"No! Don't hurt me! I'm just a child!" Sawyer cried.

"More like a baby," Alice scoffed.

"Hey, I know a fun game!" Ginger exclaimed.

"Charades?" Sawyer asked.

"No, that's dumb," Alice retorted. "Kinda like you!"

"We could play Capture the Flag," Ginger suggested.

"Does it involve making Sawyer cry?" Alice asked.

"No," Ginger replied.

"Then I don't want to play," Alice said, as she crossed her arms.

"Well then, you'll just be bored," Ginger concluded.

"Fine. We can play Capture the Flag," Alice sighed.

"Great," Sawyer said. "You two can be on a team. Donna will be my teammate."

"Okay," Alice said. She then grabbed Donna's cage and violently shook it. "Wake up, Donna! Wake up or else!"

"*Squawk!* Get your grimy mitts off of my golden cage!" Donna screeched.

"You're gonna be my partner in Capture the Flag," Sawyer informed Donna, as he opened her cage.

"Oh no! You'll get us both killed!" Donna squawked.

"Come on, Donna. Don't be a pooper. Do something super!" Sawyer begged.

"If you say that ever again, I cut your precious little chest hair clean off," Alice said grimly. Sawyer stuck his tongue out at her.

"What is chest hair?" Donna asked.

"Chest hair is..."

"Nobody cares, Sawyer," Alice interrupted, rolling her eyes.

"What about my facial hair?" Sawyer asked.

"It kinda washed off in the sea," Ginger said sheepishly.

"*Squawk!* Can we just play the stupid game already?" Donna pleaded.

"Yeah, sure," Sawyer agreed. "Everyone, hide your flag!"

"Follow me," Alice said, as she grabbed Ginger's wrist. Alice put the flag in a barrel and closed the lid. "You stay here and guard the flag."

Sawyer and Donna came onto the deck with their flag. I looked at them, rolled my eyes, and figured I shouldn't get involved. The others did the same. Donna flew up to the crow's nest at the top of the mast and placed the flag. She perched herself there and Sawyer went to find Alice's flag.

Sawyer ran below deck into the cargo hold.

"Ha!" he exclaimed. "I found your flag! I win!"

"You have to get past me to win," Alice threatened. "Ginger, go find the other flag. I'll take care of this."

"Okay!" Ginger ran away.

"Now, we can do this the easy way, or the hard way," Alice demanded.

"I choose the easy way!" Sawyer decided.

"Great, now give me your flag," Alice ordered.

"No, you give me your flag," Sawyer objected. "So then it's easy for me to win."

"No, it's supposed to be easy for me, not you," Alice argued.

"The easy way is too hard," Sawyer whined.

"Then we will fight!"

"To the death?"

"No, stupid, we'll fight to the busted lip and black eye," Alice said.

"Great!" Sawyer threw a punch at Alice. Alice, however, blocked it with one arm and grabbed Sawyer's head with the other. She then rammed Sawyer's head into her knee and hit his back with her elbow. Sawyer groaned in pain as he fell onto the floor. Alice tied him up, put her flag out of sight, and went to find Ginger. She slammed the door so hard that an oil lamp fell onto the floor.

Meanwhile, Ginger had caught sight of Donna, who was sitting on the edge of the crow's nest.

"Hey, Donna!" Ginger yelled. "I can't find your flag anywhere. Can you give me a hint?"

"*Squawk!* No, that would be stupid of a dignified bird like me," Donna answered.

"Please?" Ginger begged.

"No, this is my task; guard the flag and attack invaders," Donna squawked.

"You mean you're gonna try to hurt me if I try to win?" Ginger asked.

"*Squawk!* Yes," Donna replied. She spread her wings and looked toward the sun. "For I, Donna, whose name was derived from the Latin word *dona* meaning *gift*, named by Sydney Andrews herself, have been appointed this duty. I am now Donna the Legendary Flag Guardian, and I will take down whoever stands in the way of victory!"

"Hey, Ginger! Did you find the flag?" Alice asked.

"No," she answered. "It's nowhere, and Donna won't help me."

"Of course not. Donna would kill for victory," Alice told her. "Look, I bet it's up there, in that big basket-lookout thingy."

"No...it's not up here! *Squawk!* We didn't hide it inside the crow's nest leaving me to guard it, knowing we had an advantage," Donna said defensively.

"Alright, listen to me," Alice whispered, turning towed Ginger. "I want you to distract Donna while I get the flag. Got it?"

"How do I do that?" Ginger whispered.

"Get her to brag about herself. It's her main hobby," Alice suggested.

"Okay," Ginger whispered.

"Hey, I'll be right back," Alice said, winking at Ginger.

"Oh... yes," Ginger agreed. "Oh how bored I am now! Oh, look... an impressively beautiful parrot! Hello, Donna... um... I am very... very curious about parrots. Can you tell me about your... um..." Ginger tried to think of something to say.

"Oh, yes! *Squawk!* I have flown through many a storm, have sung many songs, and have even fallen in love."

"Um... sure... tell me about your love life," Ginger requested.

"*Squawk!* Well, you seem a little young for that..."

"No! No! Tell me about something else!"

"No, it's too late. I will just tell you about Princesse!" Donna flew down to tell Ginger her story. "*Squawk!* It was last spring. I had flown away to Parrot Island in search of a boyfriend... Hey, what are you looking at?" Donna turned around. A rope was dangling behind her.

"The rope's just moving because... I tugged it!" Ginger ran to the rope and violently tugged at it. "See!"

The rope fell from the mast. Donna looked awkwardly looked at Ginger and said, "But how did you shake that rope if it's over here and you were over there?"

"With... with my... mind! I can move things with my mind!" Ginger exclaimed.

"*Squawk!* Prove it!" Donna commanded.

"You don't believe me?"

"Not until you prove it," Donna stuck her beak in the air.

"Okay then... I will move that leaf!" Ginger proclaimed. Then she closed her eyes and crossed her fingers. Suddenly, a small gust of wind blew across the deck, carrying the leaf a few feet. Ginger opened her eyes and gasped.

"*Squawk!* Wow! You do have magical powers!" Donna exclaimed.

"Yeah..." Ginger said, at length.

"We should tell everyone! *Squawk!* All hail Queen..."

"Alright, that's it!" Ginger interrupted. "I have to tell you the truth. I don't have magical powers. I'm just a normal girl. I've never told one single lie in my whole entire life. Please forgive me! Please!"

After a minute Donna, who was oblivious to anything Ginger had said, shouted, "You're a Jedi!"

"No! That's not even a thing yet! Oh, I'm such a terrible person!" Ginger sobbed.

"Shut up, Jedi. That's getting annoying," Donna turned around. As Alice grabbed the flag, Donna tried to stop her.

"Ha! Loser!" Alice bragged.

"Give it back!" Donna screeched. She tugged at Alice's shirt with her beak, trying to throw her off of the mast.

"Hey, back off!" Alice screamed as she grabbed Donna's wings.

"*Squawk!* Let go of me!" Donna suddenly bit Alice's arm. Alice, who was in pain, let go of Donna angrily.

"Oh, so you wanna play that game, huh? Alright, let's play!" Alice yelled. Alice grabbed Donna and rammed her against the mast. Donna became so furious that she bit Alice in the arm over and over.

"Okay, that's enough! Stop it!" Alice cried painfully.

"I will not! *Squawk!* I am the Legendary Flag Guardian, and I will kill whoever gets in my way!"

"It's just a stupid game, Donna! Stop acting like a psycho!" Alice sobbed. She ran to the end of the beam to climb down, but there was no rope.

"*Squawk!* There's no escape now, loser!" Donna cackled.

"Ginger, why'd you have to pull the rope down?" Alice screamed.

"I was just trying to help!" Ginger yelled.

"Donna's about to murder me and no, you did not help!" Alice shouted.

At first, I just assumed they were all playing and exaggerating. When I turned around, I was horrified to see Ginger in tears, Alice drenched in blood, and Donna going mentally insane. I felt terrible for not checking on them sooner, but I had just never associated blood with Capture the Flag.

"Alice, we're coming!" I screamed. Ryker and I ran to the mast and climbed up to where Alice was. I grabbed Donna and pulled her away from Alice. She tried to attack me. I pinned her to the mast and tried to hold her still.

"Belle, she's crying what do I do?" Ryker asked.

"Just a second, I'm a little busy," I said.

"Umm... I think she just forgot how to breathe," Ryker said worriedly.

"Then remind her how to breathe, or something!" I demanded.

"Okay, and how do I get her down from here?" Ryker asked.

"Hey, Michael!" I yelled. "Toss us that rope!"

"Got it!" Michael exclaimed. He grabbed the rope and threw it a few feet into the air... not high enough. He tried again, but that pathetic little boy could not throw that rope to save his life.

"I'll get it," Ryker sighed, but as he stepped away Alice grabbed him and screamed in tears.

"Michael, you'll just have to come up here and give it to us," I ordered.

"I can't just climb up there!" Michael objected.

"I can!" Sydney exclaimed.

"Michael, why are you weaker than your girlfriend?" I scoffed.

"I am not!" Michael argued.

"Oh wait," Sydney said. "I climbed *that* mast. This one's too high."

"Can someone please just give us the rope?" I snapped.

"I know someone who can climb!" Sydney clapped her hands and ran to her room. She came back with Jerry.

"Jerry, go give the ugly guy this rope," Sydney said sweetly.

Jerry, who apparently wasn't just a stupid little rodent, scurried up the mast and brought the rope to Ryker. Ryker reluctantly took it and Alice was able to climb down. Once Donna had finally calmed down, Ryker and I descended onto the deck.

"Alice, are you okay?" I asked.

"Oh, your poor thing!" Sydney cried.

"I'm… I'm okay," Alice sniffled.

"Oh, so now she's okay," Ryker said as he rolled his eyes.

"I was in a panic, dummy!" Alice retorted.

"Hey, I hate to interrupt like this, but does anyone else smell smoke?" Michael asked. "And come to think of it, where's Sawyer?"

"Oh no," Alice whispered anxiously.

Into the Flames

Alice ran below deck to the cargo hold. I ran after her and found her banging on the door in tears. I suddenly heard a muffled scream from inside.

"Alice... what happened to Sawyer?" I asked anxiously.

"I... I... I'm sorry..." Alice sobbed.

"About what?" I yelled.

"I tied him up, locked the door, and I think the oil lamp fell," Alice cried.

"You mean the oil lamp that was lit?"

Alice nodded in tears.

"So you mean to tell me that you started a fire in the cargo hold, tied Sawyer up, and locked him inside?" I yelled.

"I'm sorry, okay!" Alice sobbed.

"We have to get him out of there now!" I demanded. I kicked at the door over and over, but it was too heavy. It wouldn't budge. I ran to the deck to get Ryker.

"Sawyer's about to burn to death in the cargo hold and the door's stuck!" I screamed.

"What? Let me see!" He pushed past me to see what was going on.

"It's too heavy to break down and I can't open it from out here. I'm gonna shoot it," Ryker decided.

"Then you'll just shoot Sawyer!" I panicked.

"No, I won't. And it's the only way to get to the lock," he said.

"What do you want me to do?" I asked.

"Go get water to douse the fire," Ryker told me.

"Okay," I said. I ran to find some buckets and filled them with seawater. Sydney and Michael came to help. We suddenly heard a gunshot. I rushed to the cargo hold with the others following close behind. When we arrived, Ryker opened the door and huge flames burst out of the doorway. It was worse than I had imagined. The whole room was almost consumed by fire and smoke.

"I'm going in," Ryker said hesitantly.

"No, I'll do it," I objected. "Your life's at stake. I can't lose you!"

"Belle, I know you can do it," Ryker assured me. "But that idiot is practically my brother. I have to save him. And I can't lose you, either. I love you."

"I love you, too," I said. I understood his point, and there was no time to argue with him. After pouring the water onto the flames in the doorway, I left to refill the buckets. We did this over and over, but the flames were unquenchable. I suddenly heard a loud crash and a painful shout.

"Ryker!" I screamed. I tried to run in after him, but Sydney grabbed my wrist and held me back.

"Belle, stop it! You'll get yourself killed!" she demanded.

"Oh, not this again, Sydney," I argued. "Just let me save him, for crying out loud!"

"No! You'll die if you go in there!" Sydney objected.

"And they'll die if I don't!" I yelled, as I pulled myself away from Sydney. I ran into the fire and looked anxiously for Sawyer and Ryker. I could hardly see through the smoke and flames. It was scorching hot and the air was hardly breathable. I suddenly found Sawyer lying on the floor, unconscious. He was on the brink of suffocating.

I looked over and found Ryker. It looked like three shelves had fallen on top of him, and he couldn't move. As I lifted one of the boards, Ryker suddenly said. "No, get... get Sawyer first."

"But what about you?" I asked.

"He… he's about to die… and I can… I can wait," Ryker stammered.

"I understand, I'll save him first. I'll be right back," I told him. I picked Sawyer up and carried him to the doorway. I was hardly able to stand. It hurt to breathe. I struggled to the door and handed Sawyer over to Sydney.

"He's hardly breathing. Help him," I ordered. I ran back into the cargo hold to save Ryker. When I found him, the boards on top of him were on fire, and he was barely awake.

"Ryker? Ryker, are you okay?" I asked as I picked up one of the boards.

"Yeah… yeah I'm just… just fine," he answered faintly.

"Don't worry, I'm getting you out of here." I picked up the last board.

"You don't have to carry me…I can… I can walk," Ryker said as he struggled to stand.

"No, you can hardly breathe, let me help you," I begged.

"You can... can help all you want, but... but I'm not gonna make you carry me out... out of here," Ryker argued. I grabbed his hand and helped him up. We began to walk toward the doorway, but I suddenly realized something and stopped.

"There's gunpowder back here," I said.

"So?"

"So if the fire gets too close to it, it'll explode," I said anxiously.

"Okay, then run," Ryker decided.

"There's no time," I told him as we began to run.

"Belle, go without me."

"Never!" I objected.

"Just go..." Ryker suddenly fell into my arms. Before I could think anything about it, the gunpowder exploded with a loud bang that made the *Pegasus* tremble. Scorching heat suddenly burst out from behind me. I quickly ran to Sydney with Ryker in my arms.

"The…the gunpowder exploded and… and the ship will sink if the wood burns," I panted.

"Okay, okay," Sydney said, "but let me make sure these two idiots are alright. Michael, help her put the fire out."

"I don't know how to do that!" Michael complained.

"You literally get a bucket and pour it on the fire. That's all you have to do," I explained. "Let's go."

"But we could die if we go in there!" Michael shrieked.

"We'll also die if we don't go in there!" I yelled.

"Belle, just pouring water on the flames isn't enough anymore," Sydney realized.

"You're right," I said. Then I had an idea. If we could get the water into the cargo hold directly, without having to transport it using buckets, we could douse the fire much faster. We could make a hole in the wall and let the water in, but that would sink the *Pegasus* for sure. If we made an opening just above the water level, we could steer the ship into the waves and let the water come in. But how would we get the water out of the ship and repair the opening after that?

"Michael, I need you to make a decent-sized opening in between the deck and the water's surface in that wall," I ordered.

"Aye-aye, captain!" Michael exclaimed.

"Please don't say that ever again," I said, exasperated.

"Oh, um, okay," Michael turned and left.

I ran up to the deck and hoisted all of the sails. I went to the steering wheel and viciously turned toward the waves. The *Pegasus* would govern itself from there. I climbed onto a beam on the mast at the bottom of one of the sails. I anxiously watched as the ship drifted into the rough waters. The ship rocked and swayed in the waves.

I climbed down and hurried back to the cargo hold. I looked into the room, which was still consumed by smoke and flames. Suddenly, water came gushing in through the wall! The fire hissed and died off eventually. My heart stopped beating so rapidly, but I still hadn't caught my breath, and I wasn't going to do so, anytime soon. Now, I had to get the ship out of the waves before it flooded.

I rushed back to the steering wheel. I forced the ship to turn. It reluctantly shifted and tumbled through the waves. Suddenly, a huge gust of wind blew through the air. As the sails caught the wind, the *Pegasus* tilted to its side.

This, at least, was a problem I could fix. I just had to sail the ship in a zigzag motion to go against the wind. Not too far away was an area with fewer waves, and therefore less wind. I turned the steering wheel back and forth over and over again. The *Pegasus* swayed through the sea.

The calmer water was close by, but I wasn't sure I would make it. I hadn't caught a break since Donna's fight with Alice. I was exhausted and struggling to breathe. The smoke and fire in the cargo hold had almost suffocated me.

I wearily looked up. I had almost made it. I forced myself to stay awake. I was so close. And with one final stroke of the steering wheel, I fell to the ground in anguish.

The Biscuits Are Back

I suddenly woke up to Sydney sobbing. "Belle, please don't die! If you die, I will literally kill you! So don't you dare even think about dying on me!"

"You can't kill me if I'm already dead," I mumbled.

"Belle, nobody wants your smart-talk right now. My best friend just died," Sydney scoffed.

"What's your problem?" I asked, sitting up.

"Belle just died... Oh, hi, Belle!" Sydney exclaimed.

"You're so stupid," I joked.

"Oh, shut up," Sydney said. "I was always told to assume the worst, in case things don't turn out my way."

"That's dumb," I countered.

"No, it's not. It's life," Sydney argued.

"Yeah, but death doesn't always have to be your first assumption," I told her. "Hey, how are Ryker and Sawyer?"

"They're fine," Sydney answered. "You can go down there and see them. I'm about to make supper."

"Okay, great," I said. I got up and went below deck, where Ginger and Alice were both in tears and screaming at each other.

"You almost killed my brother!" Ginger cried.

"Yeah, you almost killed me!" Sawyer repeated.

"He could have died because of you!" Ginger continued.

"Yeah, I could have died because of you!" Sawyer added.

"It's not my fault! It was an accident!" Alice yelled.

"It's not my fault," Sawyer started. "Wait what?"

"You're a bad influence and I don't think we should be friends anymore," Ginger declared.

"Yeah, you're a bad influence…"

"Sawyer, please, I don't need your help," Ginger interrupted.

"Well, it's not my fault you're such a goody-goody!" Alice snapped.

"Alright, weirdoes, sit down," I ordered. "Where's Donna?"

"She's in your room," Ginger answered.

"I'll go get her. You stay here," I said. On my way to get Donna, I saw Ryker.

"Ryker, you're okay!" I threw my arms around him happily.

"Yeah, I'm fine," he said. "Thanks, by the way."

"For what?"

"Saving my life," Ryker said. "How did you miss that?"

"I don't know," I replied. Ryker looked at me and smiled. I smiled back, just before he kissed me.

"I have to go find Donna," I said, at length. I turned and left, blushing a little. I went into my room and grabbed Donna's cage.

"*Squawk!* Where are we going?" Donna asked.

"You're in trouble," I answered.

"*Squawk!* No, no! You are not my mother!" Donna argued.

"No, I'm your captain," I said.

"But I never did anything wrong. *Squawk!* I want cake!"

I set Donna's cage next to Alice and said, "Okay, so in case you didn't notice, today was a complete disaster. Hm, who should I start with? How about Donna? Alright, Donna, do you know what a game is?"

"Squawk! It's something you play!"

"Yeah, and playing does not mean killing. So, don't try to murder someone if it's just a game. Capture the Flag should not be a matter of life and death."

"Squawk! You're a loser! I would make an *L* with my fingers, but I don't have any!" Donna retorted.

"Alice," I said, "I know the fire was an accident, but you have got to be more careful. You know Sawyer is weak and stupid. Don't go so hard on him! And next time you hear something shatter, check to make sure it's not a lamp!"

"Ginger," I continued, "next time someone is being attacked by a parrot, try to help them, or get help, but don't just stand there and cry about it. Crying doesn't help, understand? And another thing, Alice didn't mean to cause so much trouble, so give her a break. And Sawyer…"

"Oh, come on!" Sawyer whined, "What did I do?"

"Sawyer, an eight-year-old girl should not be able to beat you up. No offense, but you're pathetic! If this happens again, you won't be allowed to help us fight Clark."

"But I'm a man! I have one..."

"Nobody cares about your stupid chest hair!" Alice screamed, as she slapped Sawyer across the face.

"Hey, supper's ready." Michael walked through the door. "Um, what are you doing?"

"We're punishing Sawyer for being a wimp," I replied.

"And so you're beating him?" Michael asked, shocked.

"No, we're beating him because he won't stop bragging about his chest hair!" Alice declared.

"Don't you all think it's a little unnecessary to beat a child, just for bragging?" Michael argued.

"Oh, Alice is a walking disaster. This is kinda her hobby," Ryker added as he approached Michael. "Hey, Alice, try not to hurt him. He's small, weak, and a terrible fighter."

"Fine, whatever!" Alice let Sawyer go.

"Can we eat now?" Michael asked.

"Yeah, let's go," I said. We walked up onto the deck, where there was an old table with a set of mismatched chairs.

"Isn't the table supposed to be below deck?" Michael inquired.

"Well, we used to have one below deck, but Sawyer and Alice destroyed it. So, we had to get a new one, but it wouldn't fit."

"The chairs don't match," Michael noted.

"Yes, we know," Ryker said and sat down.

"The biscuits are back!" Sydney exclaimed, as she walked up to the table.

"You sound like you're trying to advertise them," I told her.

"Hey, where's my seat?" Sydney asked.

"You can have Michael's. He can sit on the floor," I decided.

"I'll go find one," Sydney sighed. After she left, I grinned, took a bite out of a biscuit, and put it back on the platter.

Sydney came back and looked at the biscuits. She sat down and then screamed, "Sawyer, I told you not to do that! If you eat a biscuit, don't put it back on the tray! Shame on you! You are a disgrace to this crew!"

"But I didn't do it!" Sawyer said defensively.

"Then who did?" Sydney asked.

"Uh," Sawyer hesitated. "I forgot."

"Yeah, right," Sydney rolled her eyes. "Belle, what's your problem?"

I suddenly burst out laughing, after trying so terribly hard not to. Sydney looked at me, confused.

"You sound like a dying pig," Michael scoffed.

"You look like a dying pig," I returned.

"No, he doesn't!" Sydney argued.

"Yeah, he's hot!" Alice added.

"Not as hot as me," Sawyer bragged.

"Oh, shut up," Alice said.

"Alice said a bad word!" Ginger shrieked.

"'Shut up,' is not a bad word," Alice argued.

"But my parents told me not to say it," Ginger countered.

"Then don't say it," I told her.

"What about me?" Sawyer asked.

"Everything you say is dumb anyway," I said.

"I'm tired," Sydney whined.

"Then leave," Ryker said dryly.

"Could you please show some consideration, Ryker?" Michael begged. "What's wrong, my love?"

"'My love'?" Sydney shuddered. "What... why did you... why..."

"Because I love you," Michael replied, putting his hand on Sydney's shoulder.

"Don't touch me!" Sydney screamed. "You probably have biscuit crumbs all over your hands!"

"I haven't even touched one biscuit this whole time, darling," Michael countered.

"And now it's in my hair and everything!" Sydney sobbed.

"No, it's..."

"Why did you call me 'darling'?" Sydney screamed.

"Because we're a couple," Michael said, trying to stay calm.

"Since when?" Sydney yelled, as she brushed the imaginary crumbs out of her hair.

"She's acting like you," Ryker whispered.

"Shut up," I whispered back. "I don't cry over fake biscuit crumbs and pet names."

"Yeah, but I've never called you a pet name, *honey*," Ryker joked.

"Oh, that's just disgusting," I whispered.

"Sydney, calm down," Michael pleaded.

"Don't... don't... touch me!" Sydney stuttered.

"I'm sorry, my love."

Sydney instantly broke into tears.

"Is this a seizure or a panic attack?" I asked Ryker.

"It's Sydney," Ryker answered.

"Oh, please tell me what's wrong!" Michael begged. "It hurts me to see you like this."

"Biscuit... pet name... darling... crumb... biscuit," Sydney screamed, struggling to breathe.

"Please, calm down!" Michael demanded.

"Okay, Michael needs help," I said. "What do I do?"

"How should I know?" Ryker asked.

"I'll be right back. Help her," I said.

"What am I supposed to do?"

"Tell her what you would tell me," I suggested.

"Alright," Ryker walked up to Sydney and yelled, "You're not a failure, for the fifth time, and we're not going to die! Don't murder Clark!"

"Shut up, you pig!" Sydney slapped Ryker in the face. Ryker rolled his eyes and went back to his seat.

I came back with Jerry, who was anxiously trying to get away. I gave him to Sydney. "Here."

"Jerry!" Sydney exclaimed. She kissed his ugly little nose and stopped crying. Everyone sat down and stared at Sydney in shock.

"What, you've never gotten biscuit crumbs in your hair before?" she asked nonchalantly.

"There were no crumbs," Michael told her.

"Oh," Sydney said. "Well, I'm fine, then."

"Great," Ryker said. "Hey, Sydney! Catch!"

Ryker suddenly threw a biscuit at Sydney. It hit Sydney, who screamed and fell out of her chair. I tried to hold back my laughter.

"Sydney!" Michael helped Sydney up. "Sydney, are you okay?"

"No!" Sydney walked towards Ryker. "Shame on you, Ryker Collins! Shame on you and your whole family! You are a loathsome little brat who never knows when to shut your stupid mouth!"

Sydney, somehow strengthened by her anger, grabbed Ryker's hair and pushed him over the rail into the ice-cold sea... again.

"Serves him right," Sydney declared, as she sat down. Ginger looked at her in shock and devastation.

"Sydney, you... you *killed* him!" Ginger cried.

I leaned over the rail and grabbed Ryker's hand. He was shivering and could hardly move. He was absolutely pitiful... just like the last time this happened. I left to get him a blanket and came back.

"Th... thanks," Ryker said.

"I wanna do a magic trick!" Sawyer exclaimed

"No! No magic tricks!" I protested.

"But Belle..." Sawyer groaned.

"This is a disaster waiting to happen," I argued.

"Please," Sawyer begged.

"No."

"Why not?"

"Because they never end well," I answered.

"Give me one example," Sawyer challenged.

"You got a coin stuck in Sydney's ear!" I exclaimed.

"Yeah, you did," Sydney said angrily.

"Well I won't do *that*," Sawyer assured me.

I stared at him coldly and finally said, "Fine."

"Great!" Sawyer stood up in his chair. "Who would like to be my assistant?"

"Me!" Ginger replied.

"Alrighty!" Sawyer proclaimed. "Step forth!"

"Okay!" Ginger jumped up and stood in her chair.

"Alice, bring us a blanket!" Sawyer demanded.

"Whatever," Alice sighed. She stood up and descended below deck to get a blanket.

"Now, I shall soon make Ginger disappear with my amazing magic!" Sawyer declared. Everyone rolled their eyes, as Ginger excitedly smiled.

Alice returned with a blanket. "Well?"

"Alice will now hold this blanket in front of Ginger for suspense," Sawyer directed. "Now, I will make Ginger disappear! Abracadabra!" We suddenly heard a shrill scream and a loud splash. Ginger had been pushed into the sea!

"She can't swim, you dingbat!" Alice screamed. She reached into the water and caught Ginger's hand. I came over to help Alice pull Ginger over the rail. Ginger was sobbing with fear.

"Sawyer, you just about killed your sister," Ryker said.

"No more magic tricks," I demanded.

"Sorry I almost killed you, but wasn't that such a cool trick?" Sawyer bragged.

"No!" Alice shrieked. "You know what? We're done! Come on, Ginger, let's go!"

"Supper's over," I announced, as I stood up.

"But we didn't eat anything," Michael countered.

"I don't like biscuits anymore," Sydney whined.

"I know, your cooking stinks," Ryker scoffed as he threw the biscuits into the sea.

"Ryker, I'm still hungry!" Sawyer complained.

"Too bad," Ryker said. "Let's go."

I went back to my cabin and the others went below deck. The day was over. No more parrot attacks, fires, or magic tricks. It was official: biscuits were banned from the *Pegasus* from that point on.

One of Us

I awoke around midnight to the howling wind and the creaking ship. I stayed in my hammock for a minute, listening to the sounds I had known all my life. I had heard them enough to become acquainted with them. I loved these sounds enough to stay awake for them. Falling asleep would be like walking away from someone trying to speak to you, so I listened to what I felt was like music.

I turned my head and looked at the wall. The one across from me was almost bare. I thought of possibly using one of Sydney's paintings to fill the space. I then remembered the portrait of my parents. I missed them. I never knew I could miss someone I had never known. It wasn't the same as someone leaving you, leaving a place empty in your heart that they had once filled. No, this was more like a longing. That special place in my heart was not at a loss, because it was empty from the start.

That place on the wall was as empty as the place in my heart. I finally decided that if I longed for them so much, then why not fill that space with their portrait? There was no good reason not to.

I had been awake too long to fall asleep after that. So, I got up and opened my door. The crisp air blew across my face. I shivered and closed my door. I was wide awake now. I changed into something I would have worn on any normal day, but with a black leather coat.

I stepped outside again and breathed in the freezing air. It even smelled cold. My braid blew freely in the sharp wind. There were no stars, only clouds. I almost thought it would snow, but that was unlikely.

I went below deck to find the chest with the portrait inside. I looked at it for a while and then caught sight of a note at the bottom of the chest. I picked it up and read:

Dear Belle,

I am so sorry that everything turned out this way. I want the best for you, but I cannot stay here. Not anymore. Clark has done terrible things to me and my son, and I am fearing for my life.

However, I have done whatever I can for your well-being in preparation for my departure.

Your mother has always been so kind to me, and I wanted to do this in return. Inside this chest are all of your parents' most treasured belongings. I hope that when, and if, you read this, you'll have something to hold on to, since you don't have much.

As for your education, you won't be able to learn much. I was able to teach a young boy named Dylan reading, writing, and some Biblical matters, and hopefully, he has taught you. I am already aware that you will not be like other children, but I truly want the best for you.

For my safety, I cannot give you my identity. All I can say is that I was once the wife of Clark Teach. However, it's obvious now that he never loved me or my son. If you ever find my identity by some miraculous chance, feel free to find me if you need me. However, that is quite unlikely.

I didn't blame the writer, whoever she was. She couldn't stay to take care of me, that would have gotten her and her son killed. But I almost wished she had stayed. As far back as I remembered I had been abused and tortured by Clark. But he had done even worse things to his wife, so I held nothing against her.

The door suddenly opened and Michael tip-toed in. I turned around.

"What are you doing in here?" I whispered.

"Not sure," he replied. "I couldn't sleep. The wind and creaking are too loud. I'm not used to it."

"Of course, you're not," I sighed. "You grew up in a mansion with everything you could have ever wanted."

"You say it as though it offends you."

"No, you're just a sensitive wimp," I countered. I picked up the portrait and began to make my way toward the door.

"Oh please, everyone knows that you hate me," Michael said.

"I'm not supposed to like you, am I? I have a boyfriend already, and you're just annoying."

All of a sudden, the ship violently jolted. I fell to the ground and the door slammed shut.

"You know, you could have caught me, or something," I told Michael.

"But you already have a boyfriend," Michael mocked.

"If someone is falling, you're supposed to catch them. If you don't, then you're kind of a jerk," I said with frustration.

"As much of a jerk as you are? I doubt it," Michael scoffed.

"I'm sorry, did you just call me a jerk?" I snapped. "I have done so much for you. I've given you food and a place to stay. I let you tag along, even though you have absolutely nothing to offer. I hardly ever make you work. A shark almost killed me because of you and I never even punished you!"

"And yet, you still hate me," Michael argued.

"I don't hate you!" I yelled.

"I'm leaving," Michael said, He viciously tugged at the door, but it wouldn't budge. He lost his grip on the handle and fell.

"It's stuck," he panted.

"No, you're just weak," I rolled my eyes. I gripped the door's handle and pulled with all of my strength. To my astonishment, it really was stuck.

"Go ahead, say it," Michael provoked.

"The door's stuck," I grumbled.

"I'm sorry, what was that? I couldn't hear you," Michael taunted.

"*The door is stuck!*" I screamed.

"You didn't need to shout," Michael retorted.

"It's like you *want* me to punch you!" I yelled.

"Oh, so now you're going to punch me. Great."

"I never said that."

"I cannot wait to get out of here," Michael sighed.

"Why? Am I that repulsive?" I asked angrily.

"Yes! This place is like a prison with you around!" Michael complained.

"You're not that pleasant either, you know," I returned.

"Alright, I have to know," Michael cried. "Why do you hate me so much?"

"I don't!" I denied.

"Oh, please. We all know that you have something against me. I'd at least like to know what it is," Michael pleaded.

"Why would I tell you?"

"I want to know what I'm doing wrong," Michael begged.

"Fine," I sighed after a minute. "I'm jealous. I shouldn't be, but I am."

"Jealous of what?" Michael inquired.

"You just don't get it, do you?" I started. "Alright, I'll start from the beginning. Aside from you, everyone on this ship is missing something or someone or is broken in some way. Think about it. Ryker was never loved, Alice was never wanted, and Sydney was never accepted. Ginger and Sawyer lost their parents and are orphans now. I've always been an orphan and was abused for most of my childhood. And then *you* show up. You, who has everything in the world. Michael, we came here because we had nowhere else to go. When I said our mothers weren't there to hold us back, they were either dead, or they just left. We cling to each other because we've lost everything else. But you, you already have riches, a noble family, and all the protection and security you could ever need. You don't *need* to be a Stowaway. And I know I shouldn't, but I almost feel mocked that you barged in and acted like you belong here. You already have a life. You don't *need* this one."

"What life?" Michael countered. "I had no life in London."

"How so?"

"Well, let's just be honest," Michael began. "I'm small. I'm weak. We all know it's true. And my parents, they were the worst of all. They were always peering over my shoulder, trying to protect me from nothing.

Up until I ran away, they always treated me like a child, an infant. They would say things like, 'Don't overwork yourself, honey,' and, 'Don't go over there, you could hurt yourself.' When you told me that my mother was holding me back that night at the ball, I did believe you. Everyone's always thought that. You were the first to actually say it."

"I still don't understand what you could possibly want from me," I said.

"What I'm trying to say is that I'm tired of being pampered and looked after all of the time. I want to be one of you. I want to be free. I want... no, I *need* to be with Sydney. I love her with all my heart. The only thing standing in between us was my parents, so I had no choice but to run from them. As long as they're holding me back, I have no potential."

"So, you're not afraid, then?" I asked.

"No, believe me, I am," Michael admitted. "But I'm even more afraid of what would have happened had I stayed in London."

"That's legit," I agreed. "But being one of us is a huge commitment. You're not a stuck-up little rich boy anymore, okay? You're a pirate, now. Deal?"

"Deal," Michael confirmed. I spat on my hand and held it out. Michael looked at me as though I were crazy.

"It's a hand. You're supposed to shake it," I scoffed.

"I know," Michael shuddered. "I just…"

"What, did your mother tell you you'd get germs or something?" I joked.

"Yes." Michael stepped back.

"Shake it, or you're not a Stowaway," I demanded.

"But I thought I was already a Stowaway," Michael argued.

"Just shake my hand, for crying out loud!" I begged.

"Fine," Michael repulsively shook my hand but instantly jerked away and whined, "Oh, that's gross! Why did I do that? Oh, it's disgusting! Blah! Blah!"

"Wait," I broke in. "I hear something."

"There's no such thing as ghosts, Ginger," we heard Alice say.

"Then who's in there?" Ginger peeped.

"None of your business, let's go," Alice said.

I suddenly called, "Wait! Come back!"

"Ghost!" Ginger shrieked.

"No, it's just me and Michael! The door's stuck! We're trapped!" I yelled.

"Whoever keeps yelling, will you please just shut up?" Sydney screamed, frustrated.

"Can somebody please get us out of here?" I begged.

Sydney kicked the door.

"The door's stuck," she sighed.

"What the heck is everyone doing up at *midnight?*" Ryker inquired.

"Ryker, I came in here to get something and then Michael showed up because he couldn't sleep and was bored, or something. The ship rocked and now the door's stuck," I shouted.

"Okay, I'll get it," Ryker said.

That instant, the *Pegasus* violently jerked back. I tripped and fell into Michael's arms as the door opened.

"Why are you kissing my boyfriend?" Sydney shrieked.

Cold Hearted

"When did I ever kiss him?" I asked.

"Well, you were obviously about to kiss him!" Sydney accused.

"Oh, just shut up for once, Sydney," Ryker pushed past Sydney and came to me.

"I despise Michael! And I would never kiss his gross little lips!" I said in defense.

"Then why was he holding you like that?" Sydney demanded.

"So that she wouldn't fall. I was only being polite, my love," Michael answered.

"I am not 'your love!' Sydney objected.

"But I do love you!" Michael assured her.

"Sydney, you're not actually being serious, are you?" I asked.

"No, I am being completely serious! You and Michael kissed!" Sydney exclaimed.

"No, they didn't!" Ryker yelled.

"They did, too, and you know it!" Sydney shouted.

"No, we did nothing of the sort!" Michael promised.

"Liar!" Sydney screamed.

Sydney continued to scream and yell about something that had never even happened. Maybe she was just anxious about her relationship, or maybe she'd gone completely insane. I honestly couldn't tell. But as Sydney's furious voice grew louder, so did the wind. As I listened I realized that this was no longer just wind; a storm was coming.

"Alright, we can settle all of this later," I chimed in. "Everyone, get dressed. I need to check something."

"But it's still night," Ginger said.

"Yeah, but we need to be awake if a storm comes," I told her. I ran to the upper deck. As I arrived, the cold wind howled viciously. Storm clouds loomed in the dark sky. The waves turned restlessly. I looked around and shivered. The air was almost too cold to breathe. The freezing air almost felt like it would pierce my skin.

I stared into the distance. Through the mist and clouds, I suddenly saw a spark. Lightning. Not even a second after, followed the malicious rumble of thunder. The storm was close. The wind mourned in the sharp air.

I ran back to the crew and commanded, "Everyone, onto the deck! Hurry up!"

After we had all arrived on the deck, I ordered, "Alright, the sails need to be rolled up!"

"Well, why'd you have to leave them out in the first place?" Sydney broke in.

"The wind was going in the right direction. Don't interrupt," I answered. "As I was saying…"

"Fun fact: the wind changes directions sometimes!" Sydney said.

"I said not to interrupt. Now, shut up, Sydney," I continued. "All of the sails need to be rolled up. I need everyone to help, *Sawyer*. We need to be fast. The storm's coming."

"Who said we had to listen to you?" Sydney scoffed.

"I did. Now get to work," I demanded. Sydney reluctantly went to the foremast and Michael followed after her. Ryker and I hurried to the mainmast. Alice, Ginger, and Sawyer took the one in the back.

There were only two sails on every mast. Easy enough. I quickly climbed the rigging to the highest sail on the mainmast. It took a while, however, because it was growing more and more cold with every passing minute. The wind groaned. The spars and beams creaked. The air was restless, jerking icy wind this way and that.

I finally reached the sail and began to untie it from the spar. But as I reached out towards the ropes, I began to feel rain. No, not rain… not snow, either. It must've been sleet. Struggling, I inched across the beam and at last came to the final knot. The waves roared. The *Pegasus* swayed. The ship suddenly lurched to the side. My feet slipped, as I grabbed the rope and held on with all of my strength.

"You okay?" Ryker yelled.

"Yep, just fine," I replied. I swung my legs onto the beam and climbed over. After I regained my balance, I untied the last rope. The sail flew upward into the harsh wind. I made my way to the top of the sail. When I arrived, I climbed onto the spar and began to roll up the sail. My fingers ached from the cold. They'd turned into shades of red and purple... maybe even blue. The ropes felt like they would cut my dry skin. Nevertheless, I continued to tie the sail to its beam.

I finally finished. As I made my descent, I yelled, "I'm gonna go help Sawyer. You can help Sydney when you're done."

"Got it," Ryker shouted.

I ran to the other mast and began to climb. I reached the bottom of the sail and realized that he hadn't even untied the first knot. He was just mindlessly fiddling with the rope.

"Sawyer, what are you doing?" I demanded.

"I'm untying this knot, doofus," Sawyer answered.

"No, you're not," I said, as I took hold of the knot and untied it.

"Wow, how did you do that?" Sawyer asked with amazement.

"Like this." I carefully untied a second knot, as Sawyer watched intently.

"Oh! I get it. The bunny goes around the tree and back into the hole," Sawyer declared.

"That's for tying shoes!" I screamed.

"Same thing!" Sawyer argued.

"Alright, get out of my way!" I pushed Sawyer aside and began to untie the knots. When I untied the last one, I heard a squeal. I turned around to find that Sawyer had been hanging on to the sail when it had been released from the spar.

"Sawyer, what is your problem?" I shrieked.

"I'm flying!" Sawyer exclaimed.

"If you don't get down from there you'll be *dying*!" I yelled.

"I've always wanted to ride on a magic carpet!" Sawyer cheered.

"Get back here right now!" I ordered.

"How do you expect me to do that?" Sawyer asked.

"Wait 'til the wind changes," I said. Not long after, the wind's direction shifted. As the sail glided back to me I shouted, "Sawyer, grab my hands!"

"Hey! You took my magic carpet!" Sawyer whined.

"And you'll be glad I did," I said. I climbed a little higher and began to roll up the sail. But now the freezing air was practically torturing me. I could handle pain. I'd been beaten, cut, bruised, and broken my whole life. But this was unlike any other pain I'd ever experienced. It felt as though the air itself was biting me, nipping at my skin. My fingers were numb and cracked from the dry skin. It was hard to breathe and hard to move. It wasn't pain, it was captivity. The icy wind had taken me as its victim.

I tied the last knot and was done. I began to climb down but suddenly heard a shrill cry. I looked up and saw that Michael was hanging from a beam. I soon realized that the beam had become frozen. Michael must have slipped. Now, he was struggling to hold on and screaming for help.

"Sydney!" Michael called. "Sydney, hand me the rope!"

"Who says I have to?" Sydney scoffed.

"Please! I can't hold on much longer!" Michael cried.

"I'll get it." Ryker stood up to help Michael. He had gone to help Michael and Sydney earlier and was on the other end of the spar.

"No, you don't have to," Sydney told Ryker.

"I'm begging you! If you don't help me, I could die!" Michael pleaded.

"Well, then, you can die, for all I care!" Sydney snapped.

Ryker picked up the rope to help Michael. Sydney, in her vicious anger, grabbed his shoulders and stopped him.

"You know you're just like me," she whispered. "You know you'll never be good enough for the one you love. You know they love someone else. You know they don't really want you. Don't deny it, Ryker. *You're just like me.*"

Sydney took Ryker's hands and looked into his eyes with malice. Then all of a sudden, she kissed him. I stared in shock. My best friend in the whole world had just betrayed me. I looked at Michael, whose tears had frozen on his cheeks. His hands faltered. Every waking second brought him closer to death.

Ryker, in a violent rage, punched Sydney in the nose. Sydney wailed in pain, but no one pitied her, not after what she'd done. Ryker tossed Michael the rope. Michael reached to grab it.

His fingers shook as he held on to the beam. The rope flew past his hand. Michael failed to reach it. His finger gave way and slipped. And as Ryker reached out to save him, Michael fell into the sea.

Michael immediately drifted back in the waves. My first impulse was to jump in and save him, so I did. The icy cold water felt as though would tear my skin off. I opened my eyes and grabbed Michael's arm. I could hardly move, at this point. I'd struggled back to the ship, where I took Ryker's hand. He pulled the two of us over the rail.

Ryker took Michael from me and carried him to the hold, where there were some blankets stored. The rest of the crew followed him, no one noticing I had stayed put. I was so cold I couldn't move at all. I was too numb to even try if I wanted to. I suddenly lost the little trace of strength I had left and fell to the ground, shaking and crying helplessly.

Ryker emerged from below deck and ran towards me. I wearily looked up at him.

"Why didn't you come with us?" he asked, as he helped me up.

"I... couldn't." I shivered.

"I'm so sorry. I should've made sure you were okay," Ryker said.

"No… it's… it's fine," I stammered.

"It's not fine, at all. I'm a terrible boyfriend."

"No… you were just… just trying to… to help Michael," I stammered.

"Yeah, but…"

"No… I'm fine… really," I assured him.

Ryker nodded. He led me to the cargo hold. When we finally made it, I sat against the wall. Ryker gave me a quilt and said, "You know, that was a brave thing you did out there."

"What?"

"When you saved Michael."

"Oh, I wasn't trying to be brave, or anything. It was just my first instinct to save him," I admitted.

"But you *were* brave. You've always been brave," Ryker said. "I'll be right back. There are some bandages in another room. They say they're good for frostbite."

"Okay," I said. As Ryker left I closed my eyes. I had warmed up a little and suddenly realized how tired I was. Sure enough, I had already fallen asleep by the time Ryker returned.

True Love

I finally woke up, around seven o' clock in the morning. It wasn't all that pleasant, though. My neck was stiff from sleeping against the wall and my nose was stopped up from being out in the cold. I rubbed my eyes and looked around. Michael was still unconscious. Ryker was already awake and looked like he'd hardly slept through the night.

"Hey, look who finally decided to wake up," Ryker said with a smile. "You feel any better?"

"Yeah, I'm okay," I answered as I stood up.

"Do you need anything?" Ryker asked.

"No, I'm good," I replied. "But I have to go check on Donna. She's been caged up all night. She's probably gone insane by now."

"Alright," Ryker nodded. I turned to leave as he said, "Love you."

"Love you, too," I replied. "Wow, that sounded so weird."

"Yeah, that was weird," Ryker agreed.

"Yeah." I left to go to my room. I opened the door and saw that Donna was staring angrily at me.

"*Squawk! Squawk!* Bad captain! Mean captain! Uncage me! Uncage me right now," Donna screeched.

"There you go." I opened Donna's cage. "Sorry about that."

"You'd better be sorry! That's animal abuse!" Donna squawked. "I should call the cops!"

"You can't. We're in the middle of the sea," I argued. Donna defiantly stuck her beak in the air.

"*Squawk!* I'm bored," Donna complained.

"After I get dressed, I'll take you below deck," I decided.

"Below deck is a boring place," Donna objected.

"Well, I have to go check on Ryker."

"Your dumb husband is just fine without you," Donna argued.

"He's not… whatever," I sighed. I finished getting dressed, left with Donna, and went below deck into the cargo hold.

"How is he?" I asked, referring to Michael.

"Not great. I'm getting worried," Ryker said anxiously.

Suddenly, Michael sneezed and looked up at Ryker. He shakily asked, "Are you God?"

"No. You're not dead!" Ryker said sharply.

"Oh." Michael sat up.

"*Squawk!* I'm back! Hey, who's that?" Donna asked, as she perched on my arm.

"She… she… she *talks?*" Michael gasped.

"Sadly, yes," Ryker said.

"Hey, you're not all that pleasant, either!" Donna snapped.

"Where is Sydney?" Michael asked, as he stood up.

"I'd stay away from her, if I were you," Ryker said.

"No, I must speak to her," Michael pressed.

"To tell her how bad of a girlfriend she is?" I assumed.

"No. She's not okay. I want to check on her," Michael said.

"Has Sydney ever been okay?" Ryker scoffed.

"No, I mean she's sorrowful," Michael clarified. "I must check on her."

Michael pushed past me and went to the door of Sydney's room. Taking a deep breath, he knocked quietly.

"I don't want to talk to you," Sydney sniffled. "Just leave me alone."

"Please, let me in," Michael begged. "I only want to help."

"How could you possibly help?" Sydney opened the door. Her face was blemished with one black eye, a busted lip, and a bruised nose. After a minute she said, "You caused all of this."

"If you would just listen…"

"There's nothing you have to say that's worth listening to," Sydney objected.

"Please, Sydney, I love you."

"No, you don't!" Sydney cried. "You love Belle!"

"You know that's anything, but true!" Michael yelled.

"You kissed her!"

"Sydney, that is not what happened! Please, just listen to me for one moment. The ship jerked back, and

Belle tripped. I caught her. That is all that happened," Michael said. "Sydney, I love you with my whole heart. I would do anything for you. I would never betray you. At the ball, I promised you I'd always be with you. And I will keep that promise as long as I live. I've made it clear that I love you, but you won't accept it. You won't believe me. I'm begging you to love me, *please*. And I know you do, somewhere deep inside that complicated heart of yours, but you've changed since that night at the ball. What's wrong, really? Because I know it's something deeper than me ever cheating on you, which you know is impossible for me to do. I just don't understand. I'm sorry. I wish I did. But Sydney, why won't you love me?"

Sydney looked up at Michael in tears. After hesitating, she finally admitted, "I'm afraid to love you." She paused and sniffled "I want to love you, but if I do, I could end up heartbroken. Michael you just… you just don't understand. It's complicated. The whole time I was at that boarding school, I was made fun of and told that no one would ever love me. So, I believed them. And now that you're my… my *boyfriend*, I don't know how to accept it. Last night, I wasn't mad at *you*, I was just mad at everything in general. And I didn't trust you to love me, so I just assumed you were cheating on me and I took my anger out on you. I'm sorry, but, I mean, how do I know you love me, like really? I'd rather you just didn't love me at all than try to pretend just to make me feel good. There's nothing about me to love, anyway. It's just not realistic. It's just some stupid mind game that I've fallen into."

"That's impossible," Michael argued. "I can't help but love you."

"Why?" Sydney asked. "You have no good reason to love me."

"Yes, I do," Michael assured her.

"Yeah, right," Sydney scoffed. "I almost killed you!"

"You were upset," Michael said. "What you did wasn't okay at all, but you had your reasons, even if they weren't good ones."

"That doesn't change anything. You almost died because of me. You don't have to love me. You deserve better."

"But I forgave you. Love keeps no record of wrongs, remember?"

"I never said I wanted to be forgiven!" Sydney shouted.

"Why would you not want to be forgiven?" Michael asked.

"Because I'm too late for your mercy!" Sydney cried. "No matter how hard I try, nothing I can ever do will make up for what happened. So don't waste your time loving a lost cause like me."

"You're not too late for mercy, and you're not a lost cause," Michael said softly. "Look at you, you're in tears. If you would please just accept the fact that I love you, I could help you. Your identity isn't determined by your flaws, it's determined by God. I just wish you could understand that."

"I don't want to accept you help," Sydney snapped.

"Then what do you want?" Michael sighed.

"To break up with you!" Sydney yelled.

"Why?"

"Because I'm not ready to love you, and I'll never be ready, because I'll never have a boyfriend!" Sydney screamed.

"So, you don't love me then?" Michael asked, heartbroken.

"I can't," Sydney replied.

"Alright then," Michael resolved. "I'll still love you, either way."

"No you won't," Sydney denied. "I broke your heart. Twice."

"I can love you with a broken heart," Michael said.

"No, you can't. I'm not the one for you, and you know it. Breaking up means moving on." Sydney shut the door. Michael stood there in shock. After a moment, he came back into the cargo hold. He sat against the wall in misery, and sighed.

"You good?" Ryker asked.

"We just broke up," Michael muttered.

"Good! You finally realized you're too good for her," Ryker declared.

"*She* broke up with *me*," Michael clarified.

"Because she still thinks you cheated on her?" I asked.

"No. She knows the truth," Michael said.

"So that nag broke up with you, for no reason?" Ryker asked.

"She's not a nag, and she had her reasons!" Michael stormed.

"What reasons?" Ryker asked.

"She's just not ready. She can't handle a relationship right now, and I respect that," Michael sighed.

"Not ready?" I asked.

"Not ready to love me," Michael said.

"Alright, that's it!" Ryker yelled angrily. "Belle, do you mind if I throw your best friend across the room?"

"Yes, I mind!" I cried.

"Fine," Ryker sighed.

"I'll go talk to her," I said. I went to Sydney's room and didn't even bother to knock. I kicked the door open and yelled, "What is your problem?"

"I'm too skeptical and I'll be single my whole life because I'm an idiot and I'll never be ready to have a boyfriend," Sydney sobbed, and she stroked Jerry's fur.

"You broke his heart," I said, as I sat down.

"I know, and he *forgave* me! He's ruining this whole thing. Why can't he just get over me?"

"He can't, Sydney. He loves you too much," I said.

"How do you know that?" Sydney cried.

"Sydney, you've hurt him so many times, and he always gives you another chance. He doesn't care what you think, he'll always love you. If that weren't true, he would have gotten over you by now."

"Oh, darn it!" Sydney cried. "That actually makes sense! Someone finally loves me, and I ruined it!"

"You didn't ruin it, you idiot," I said. "You can fix it."

"Really?" Sydney sobbed.

"Yes, but blow your nose first, 'cause you're a hot mess," I said.

"Okay," Sydney sniffled. She hugged me tightly and said, "Thank you."

"No problem," I replied. "So when you're ready, go talk to Michael."

"I will," Sydney nodded.

"Good." I left Sydney's room and went back to Michael and Ryker.

"I talked some sense into her. She's fine now," I told them.

"So she doesn't hate me?" Michael asked.

"Nope."

"If you two get back together, I'll go ahead and plan your funeral," Ryker said dryly.

"What?" Michael asked.

"You're, like, in love with Belle, so you can, like, die, for all I care!" Ryker mocked. "You…"

His words were cut off when we heard a knock at the door. Michael opened it as Ryker whispered, "She'll haunt you for the rest of your life. She's the worst girl you'll ever meet."

"Shut up," Michael mouthed.

"Um… can I… talk to you?" Sydney asked timidly.

"Of course," Michael said as he shut the door behind him.

"I… I… I, um," Sydney stuttered. She suddenly broke into tears and cried, "I… I love you, Michael. I… I've always loved you."

"I love you, too, Sydney." Michael wrapped his arms around Sydney, who was sobbing into his shoulder.

"I'm so sorry," she said, in tears.

"I forgive you. I'll always forgive you," Michael ran his fingers through Sydney's hair. She looked up at him and smiled. Knowing this wasn't a fantasy that was too good to be true, she kissed him... a real kiss, one filled with more passion than she'd ever dreamed of. Sydney had no need to doubt anymore. She knew this was a true love's kiss.

The Hydra's Revenge

We were now ten days into our voyage. I looked out onto the sea one morning, which was glimmering with speckles of blue and white, reflecting the red sunlight across a cloudless sky.

I turned around, as Ryker walked onto the deck and said with a smile, "I thought you were teaching Michael how not to get killed."

"I gave up when he almost shot me," Ryker said.

"It's not even Michael I'm worried for," I admitted. "It's Ginger. She's too afraid to fight or do anything, for that matter. She's been sheltered her whole life and she can't defend herself because she's apparently too nice."

"She'd defend Sawyer," Ryker said.

"Would she?"

"Yeah," Ryker continued. "She's selfless, she'd do anything for him."

"That's crazy," I argued.

"Oh, please, you're plenty crazy," Ryker countered.

"What? No... I'm crazy at all!"

"You tried to fight a cobra on your own and pushed me off the ship."

"It was for your own good."

"Fine, but you also got mad at me for dying."

"That's Sydney's fault!"

"You're still crazy," Ryker resolved.

"You know you love it," I said with a grin.

"Always."

I stared off into the distance and caught sight of a ship. It wasn't very far away, and from what I could tell, it had a Hydra carved into the bowsprit and black sails.

The smile on my face faded away when I realized what was going on.

"Go load the cannons. There's someone following us," I ordered.

"How do you know?" Ryker asked.

"They tried to plunder us about a year ago, remember?" I said.

"When you cut off that guy's leg?"

"Yep. I bet he wants revenge," I assumed.

"Yeah, and if he even lays a finger on you, I'll cut off the other leg," Ryker said grimly, as he left. I went below deck to find the others.

"Hey, people are trying to kill us, so you guys need to get over here and fight them off!" I yelled.

"Is it windy outside?" Sydney asked, as she came out of her room.

"A little," I replied.

"Then I'm not going. I just brushed my hair and it took me two hours. I want no business with the wind right now," Sydney scoffed.

"I don't like fighting," Ginger said.

"I do!" Alice exclaimed, as she ran out of her room with a pistol and a sword.

"Michael! Sawyer! Wake up!" I screamed, as I kicked the door open.

"Why?" Michael groaned.

"We're about to be attacked, so get up. And put a shirt on!" I said.

"Let me see! I wanna see!" Sydney shrieked.

"Good morning, beautiful," Michael said to Sydney.

"Shut up, Michael," I snapped.

Sydney, who was speechless, stared at Michael. Her eyes were almost as big as her goofy grin.

"You can swoon over your boyfriend later. Let's go," I sighed, as I dragged Sydney away from the door.

I ran back to the deck, only to find that the *Hydra* was growing closer and closer with every coming second. My heart raced. I stared at that wretched ship, knowing they'd attack any minute. I didn't dare to move when I heard the rest of the crew walking onto the deck. No one made a sound. We were ready to fight, but we were waiting. And after a moment that seemed like forever, it happened.

With a loud bang, their cannons fired. Our sails were suddenly torn apart as we fired back at the *Hydra*. That awful, gloomy ship relentlessly lurked closer. We had no choice now. We'd either fight, or die trying. I grabbed a pistol, ready to shoot at any moment.

Suddenly, the captain shouted, "Where are you, Blondie? It's about time for my revenge!"

Overtaken by anger, Ryker shot his arm. And so the fight began. The captain leaped onto the *Pegasus* and strode toward me as his wooden leg monotonously tapped the deck. I stayed put. My eyes were locked on his vicious face, which had only one eye. He had dark, tan skin and a large, muscular build.

"You're scared, aren't you?" he snarled.

"Not of *you*," I scoffed.

"I'll have your head before I leave," he said.

"Not if I fight you off."

"And how do you expect to do that?"

"Just like this!" I pulled out my sword and began to fight. The captain immediately drew his own sword to deflect mine. I couldn't make any blows at him. This combat went on and on. Neither of us had even been scratched. I couldn't just defend myself like this for hours. I had to do something... something reckless enough to hurt him.

I suddenly jumped back into the air, headfirst. As my feet came up I kicked that gruesome captain's throat. He stumbled in shock as I landed. When I stood up, I looked at those furious eyes, that blood-stained nose, and the violent blade that longed to kill me.

The captain flung his sword towards my neck and, out of some unknown impulse, I cut his hand off, which fell to the ground, still gripping the sword. I quickly took the sword and crossed both around his neck.

"Get out," I said grimly.

"Not until you're dead," the captain replied. He suddenly brought his arm up and punched me in the mouth. I fought back with both swords for what seemed like forever. But I still wasn't afraid. I had a chance. I couldn't back down now.

Meanwhile, Ginger had found herself hiding behind the iron bars of the brig. She sat there, drenched in tears and overcome by dread. Anxiously praying not to be found there, she huddled herself into the darkest corner. She knew she didn't belong on a pirate ship and cried even more at the realization that she was completely useless. She longed to return to Massachusetts, to her home and her family. Silently calling for her mother to come back for her, she sobbed to herself, alone in the cold, dreary brig.

Back on the deck, I continued to fight. The sun relentlessly burned upon my cheeks, which were covered in sweat. The captain was now weak. I had almost beat him. But that violent anger still loomed in his dark eyes. He had come to kill me, and he wouldn't give up until he'd done so.

"Not until you're dead, Blondie," he panted. As I brought up my sword he grabbed my right arm and pinned it against the rail. Then he repeated, "Not until you're dead."

With a new strength and fury, he rammed my right arm against the rail. I screamed as a bone snapped in between my elbow and my wrist. Blood streamed out of the veins that had been torn. I shakily looked up at that wretched pirate through the seething, terrible pain. I gripped my sword. I had to save myself, somehow.

"Belle!" Ryker cried as he ran toward me. Another pirate suddenly grabbed his neck and threw him onto the ground, knocking him out. Sawyer looked up at him and stopped fighting. Before he knew it, a gun had been put to his head and he was screaming for me to save him.

I didn't know what to do. If I tried to save him, I'd be killed instantly. I'd give my life for Sawyer, but I couldn't save him if I was dead. I continued to fight, hating myself for not doing anything for Sawyer, but there was nothing I could possibly do.

Ginger, who was still crying behind those cold iron bars, looked up when she heard Sawyer. He was the only one she had left to love and depend on. Her heart broke at the thought of losing him. She hated thinking of the pain he was in.

Ginger looked dismally through the bars and caught sight of a pistol. She shuddered at the idea of ever using it. But that pistol could have been what Sawyer's life depended on. Ginger slowly walked towards it and reluctantly picked it up.

She shakily climbed onto the deck and looked up at Sawyer. She raised her trembling arms. Not knowing how she could possibly do a thing like this. Ginger took a deep breath.

Then, she pulled the trigger.

The murderous pirate who had almost killed Sawyer fell to the ground with his leg drenched in blood. Ginger stood frozen in shock.

"I... I... I didn't want... he would have killed you..." Ginger stammered.

"You just kept me from dying," Sawyer said, dumbfounded.

"I couldn't lose you."

"I couldn't lose me, either."

"What?" Ginger asked.

"You wouldn't understand. I'm dumb. My brain's on a whole 'nother level," Sawyer told her.

The *Hydra's* gruesome captain barely had any strength left. Then again, neither did I. I couldn't fight much longer or I'd pass out. So, I gathered all of the strength I had, drew my sword one last time, and sliced that wretch's arm right off.

"I told you to get out," I said coldly. "I suggest you do so now if you wanna keep your other arm."

The captain stared at me with his cold, vicious eyes and reluctantly turned away. His crew followed him to board their own ship again. Once they had left, I ran back to Ryker, who was still unconscious.

"Belle!" Sydney screamed, running towards me "Your arm! It got snapped in half! Get up! Get up! I need to treat it! Nobody cares about your boyfriend right now! Get up!"

"I care," I argued. "What if he got a concussion or something?"

"He's fine," Sydney said. "Get up."

"Are you sure?" I asked worriedly.

"Positive. But you, on the other hand, have a broken arm," Sydney said.

"Yeah, but…"

"Sydney! Sydney!" Michael shrieked. "Are you okay? Are you hurt?"

"I'm okay. Is something wrong?" Sydney asked.

"No… I'm… I'm fine…"

"Oh, you poor sweet sweetheart! You're traumatized, aren't you?"

"Just a little," Michael said shakily.

"I have something that'll traumatize you!" I exclaimed, holding out my arm.

"No! Stop! Get it away! Please!" Michael cried.

"There, there. It's okay," Sydney said sweetly. "Hey, I need you to check on Ryker when he wakes up. Can you do that?"

"Yes, I will," Michael replied.

"Great. Come on, Belle," Sydney said. I followed her below deck and waited as she looked for bandages and water to treat my arm. I sat down and sighed tiredly. My arm throbbed in pain. It hurt just to look at it. I had barely survived this fight, and I began to wonder. How could I ever survive against Clark?

Secrets and Scars

Sydney soon returned with a bucket of water and some bandages. She set them on the ground and sat down in front of me, telling me to hold out my arm.

"What are you gonna do?" I asked nervously.

"I'm just gonna clean it and bandage it," Sydney answered. She dipped a cloth into the bucket of water and pressed it against my arm.

"Did you put salt in this?" I shrieked.

"Yes, to keep it from getting infected. Calm down."

"You can't just put salt in an open wound!" I objected.

"I do it all the time," Sydney said. "You're just always too knocked out to feel it."

"Well, I can feel it now!" I exclaimed.

"Does it hurt, or something?" Sydney asked.

"Yes!" I screamed.

"Then deal with it. I know what I'm doing."

"How do you know?"

"Because that's what I was taught to do. Look, I know that Dylan guy kept you alive for ten years, but he never went to school, and I did. So please just calm down and trust me."

"What does Dylan have to with any of this?"

"Didn't he take care of you and bandage your wounds, and stuff like that?"

"Every now and then," I answered, wishing Sydney hadn't brought this up.

"But I thought Clark..."

"I bandaged them myself," I said abruptly.

"Was Dylan not able to?" Sydney went on.

"Why do you need to know?" I snapped.

"Oh, I'm sorry. I didn't mean to be invasive," Sydney said. "I just thought it'd take your mind off the pain. I didn't mean anything by it, I promise."

"I know," I sighed. "You don't have to be sorry. It's okay."

"Okay," Sydney said, as she took the cloth off of my arm. "The bone's sticking out. I'll have to pop it back in."

"Go ahead and do it. Get it over with," I said.

"You sure?"

"Yep."

"Okay," Sydney said hesitantly. All of a sudden, she forcefully pushed the bone back into place.

"You didn't tell me it was gonna hurt *that* much!" I screamed.

"One of the bones in your arm snapped in half," Sydney said. "What did you expect?"

"I don't know, just not *that*!" I cried.

"I'll also have to give you stitches."

"No! I don't need stitches! I feel fine!" I objected as I stood up.

"Sit down. I'm giving you stitches," Sydney demanded.

"For this little scratch?" I said, almost too happily.

"Belle, it's not a little scratch! I can see your bones! You need stitches!" Sydney shouted.

"You can't see them if you close your eyes!" I argued.

"What is wrong with you?" Sydney screamed.

"My arm snapped in half," I answered.

"Which is why you need stitches!"

"I thought you were my friend!"

"I am your friend! Do you want to keep your arm, or not?"

"Yeah, but..."

"*Sit! Down!*" Sydney ordered.

"Fine," I muttered, as I reluctantly sat back down.

"Alright, I'm dying to know. You break your arm and act like you're just fine, but you freak out when you're around needles. Why?" Sydney inquired.

"I don't really wanna talk about it," I said.

"Okay, then." Sydney sighed.

"Find something else to talk about," I begged.

"Did you ever have a crush on Dylan?" Sydney asked.

"I meant something other than Dylan," I said grimly.

"Why not Dylan?"

"I'd just rather not talk about him right now," I answered.

"Why not?"

"Why do I have to tell you?"

"I'm just curious as to why he's such a pain to talk about," Sydney admitted. "I mean, there's obviously something wrong with him, right?"

"There's nothing wrong with him," I argued.

"Then why can't we talk about him?"

"Because I don't want to!"

"Why not?"

"Why do you care?" I yelled.

"Because it's obviously bothering you, and I wanna know what's up," Sydney replied.

"It's not a big deal or anything. You're just being nosy."

"Is Ryker jealous?" Sydney asked suddenly.

"I... I don't know," I confessed.

"I mean, I guess he would be... if you ever *did* have a crush on Dylan."

"I never had a crush on him, Sydney! He treated me like crap! He was a jerk to me!" I screamed. "There, I guess that's all you ever wanted to hear."

"No... no, I just wanted to have something to talk about. I didn't mean to upset you. I'm sorry," Sydney sighed.

"There's a reason I didn't want to talk about him," I said dismally as two tears ran down my cheeks.

"Belle... can I ask you one more thing... about Dylan?" Sydney asked timidly, after a few silent minutes.

"I'd rather you didn't," I said. "It hurts me just to think about him."

"I know. That's part of what I wanted to ask you about."

"Whatever. Go ahead," I said, as I rolled my eyes.

"I don't think we should save Dylan," Sydney admitted.

"What are you talking about?" I asked, shocked.

"He hurt you, and if you can't even think about him, what's gonna happen when he joins the crew?"

"He wasn't a bad person, Sydney," I said. "He saved my life and now I need to save his."

"But you said he was a jerk to you," Sydney argued.

"He had a short temper, that's all. It's nothing, really," I said nonchalantly.

"Okay, well, it didn't seem like *nothing* when you started crying."

"I don't want to talk about it," I murmured.

"That's okay. You don't have to," Sydney said. She finished stitching my arm and began to bandage it. I looked down at that wretched wound that she'd sown back together. Tears began to form in my eyes again as I remembered the bloody scars that I was covered in. I remembered the pain that both my heart and body had throbbed in almost every day for years. And now the awful secrets relentlessly tore through my soul, begging to come out. They couldn't be kept in any longer. I began to cry, unable to stop the battle I fought against my very heart.

"Can I trust you?" I asked abruptly.

"Yes, of course," Sydney answered gently.

"I… I lied to you," I said hesitantly. "Those scars… they're not *all* from Clark. Some… some are… they're from…"

"From who?" Sydney asked. "Don't worry, you can tell me."

"No, I can't," I sobbed. "I can't… I can't tell anyone."

"It's okay. You don't have to. But if you want to, I'll listen."

"Promise you won't tell anyone," I pleaded.

"Belle, you know I can't keep secrets," Sydney said.

"You *have* to keep this one. You're the only person I can trust," I begged.

"Why not Ryker?"

"He'll kill Dylan if he finds out," I said.

"Oh… alright, then. Tell me."

"So… you know how Dylan would get food for me… since Clark didn't feed us?" I started, with tears flowing down my cheeks. "Well, every now and then, he… he would get caught… and then beaten. I would have just gotten food for myself, but most of the time I was handcuffed in the brig, or crippled. And… and Dylan blamed me… whenever he was caught, for anything, not just food. So he took it out on me… one time he even whipped me, like the time when…" I hesitated, choked with tears. "When Dylan tried to rebel against Clark… Clark found him and gauged out one of his eyes out with a needle… and forced me to watch. But that's not the whole reason I'm afraid of needles. He took it out on me. He tried to jab one of my eyes out, Sydney. *I was nine.*"

"Oh, Belle!" Sydney stopped her work and wrapped her arms around me. "I had no idea he was… I mean, I'd always thought he was like a brother to you."

"Don't get me wrong, he was," I corrected. "He stood up for me when no one else would. Dylan's not heartless. He's not like Clark. I can't tell you how many times that man tried to murder me and Dylan saved my life. He's not a bad person, he just had some issues."

"Yeah, but if he ever hurts you, I'll hurt him," Sydney promised.

"Fine. You can't do much anyway," I joked.

"I can see why you would think that… mostly because it's true, but I'm still gonna look out for you, and when I punch him I'll try *really* hard not to miss."

"You know what?" I said with a smile. "You may be one of the most annoying people in the world, but I couldn't ask for a better friend."

"You, too, but you're not annoying," Sydney laughed. She finished bandaging my arm and put it in a sling, telling me it would be just fine. I gave Sydney one last hug and left, shocked at how I'd almost forgotten how good of a friend she was.

You Promised

I walked out to the deck to find Ryker standing on a beam, replacing one of the sails. When he looked down and saw me, his face lit up with joy. He quickly climbed down and ran to me happily.

"You scared me to death," he said. "I'm so sorry. I should've helped you."

"It's okay. I'm fine now," I assured him.

"How's your arm?"

"It feels a little better," I answered. "It's gonna take a while to heal, though. I'm hoping it gets better before we get to Crossbone Cove."

"Yeah..."

"What's wrong?"

"Nothing's wrong," Ryker answered curtly.

"Is this about Dylan again?" I inquired.

"It really doesn't matter. I don't wanna bother you with it," Ryker said.

"It matters to me. Go ahead. Tell me," I begged.

"It's kinda stupid. It's not a big deal, anyway," Ryker argued.

"If it's not a big deal, then why can't you tell me?"

"Because I don't need to," Ryker replied.

"But why *can't* you?" I asked.

"I don't wanna upset you, that's all."

"I won't be upset."

"Yes, you would."

"Tell me," I pleaded.

"It'd be better for both of us if I didn't," Ryker objected.

"You promised you wouldn't keep any secrets from me," I urged, just before realizing the fact that I was also keeping a secret.

"Yeah, but…"

"Tell me," I demanded.

"It's not important, and it won't sound right, no matter how I say it."

"You promised," I said, remembering that I had made the same promise. Was I doing something wrong by not telling Ryker about Dylan? No… of course not. I was only trying to protect Dylan.

"If I tell you, I could hurt you," Ryker said, almost angrily.

"I don't care about that," I argued.

"Fine… just promise you'll hear me out. It's not what it sounds like."

"Of course," I said with a nod.

"So… you know I love you," Ryker began. "And you know I want what's best for you. And I want you to have what you deserve…"

"Yes, I know."

"Well, maybe that's not me," Ryker admitted.

"What are you talking about?" I asked.

"Belle, you know what I'm talking about," Ryker sighed. "You're amazing, in every way possible. And I love you to death… but you deserve better."

"Better?"

"Someone better than me."

"And you think this 'someone' is Dylan, don't you?" I said angrily. "You're gonna break up with me because you think I'm better off with *Dylan*?"

"I never said I wanted to break up with you," Ryker said.

"Then why do you think I deserve to be with Dylan?" I yelled.

"Because I have nothing to offer you, Belle. And Dylan's done so much for you. I'm holding you back."

"From what?" I asked furiously.

"A better life!" Ryker answered.

"*What* better life?" I screamed.

"One with Dylan!"

"Ryker, you promised you'd always be with me."

"I just want what's best for you."

"Then why are you doing this to me?" I cried.

"If you would just listen…"

"Shut up! Just shut up!" I yelled, as I pushed past Ryker and stormed off to my room.

"Belle, please…"

"I'm not talking to you."

"Why?"

"Because you're and jerk, and I hate you!" I screamed as I slammed my door.

"Belle! Belle!" Ryker yelled as he banged on the door. "I'm sorry! Open the door! Please! I'm sorry!"

I refused to say anything. I sat against the door and stared dismally across the room. I felt as though my heart had been stabbed by the boy I loved more than hardly anything in the whole world. I had put all of my trust and hope into him, only to find that he would willingly give me away... to Dylan. Had I been living a lie, since the moment I first saw him? I loved Ryker with all of my heart, and I'd always assumed we were meant for each other. Was I wrong to think that? Maybe I was.

"Why didn't I just tell him Dylan was a jerk?" I thought. "I shouldn't have to tell him, that's why. He should love me either way. And no, what he did to me was not out of love. He thought he could offer me a 'better life' by breaking up with me. It's not my fault he's insecure. Plus, boys are supposed to be jealous, aren't they? Ryker shouldn't be *okay* with the thought of losing me. Unless I really am worth nothing to him, and he's been acting this whole time. Now, that's just crazy. Of course, Ryker loves me. Yeah, right. That ship has sailed."

"*Squawk!* Don't be so upset, Belle," Donna said suddenly. "Lots of people get divorced. What happened? Was your stupid husband being mean to you? Learn to live with it. Boys never grow up."

"I don't wanna talk to you right now," I mumbled.

"*Squawk!* I didn't ask what you wanted!"

"I'm not gonna pour out my feelings to a parrot," I scoffed.

"Uncage me! I'll teach Ryker a lesson! A violent lesson!" Donna screeched.

"It's not your problem," I said coldly.

"Fine! Sit here in your infinite misery! You know, you're gonna regret not letting me beat up your husband!" Donna squawked. "He's a real dork, and you know it! Admit it! *Squawk!* Admit it! Admit it! Admit it!"

"Can you please just shut up?" I snapped.

"No! I can't! Cake! Cake! Cake! Cake!"

"I told you to shut up!" I yelled.

"No, you asked!" Donna taunted.

"Shut up!" I screamed, as I took Donna's cage, threw it outside, and slammed my door. I stood motionless in front of my door, too hurt to feel any pain, too depressed to feel any sadness. I didn't want to think, but that was all I could do now.

Ryker didn't love me anymore. No, instead of loving me, he left me so that I could have Dylan, the boy I dreaded thinking of. Ryker promised he would always be with me. I should've known it wasn't true. But he was so perfect. He was flawless in every way possible. I didn't even know he was capable of breaking my heart. My first reaction to heartbreak had always been going to Ryker. But I couldn't now. He was gone. I was alone.

And yet I couldn't stop loving him. I wanted to run back into his arms, but I couldn't. Even then, I still would've given my life for him, and I hated it. I hated being in love, I hated Ryker, and I hated myself.

I fell to the ground in misery and found myself sobbing on the floor. My whole life had fallen apart so suddenly. Everything had been perfect this morning, and now all of that perfection was only a memory.

Choked with tears, I hopelessly whispered, "You promised."

I Can't Leave You

I didn't know how long I'd been lying on the floor. The sound of thunder finally brought me out of that awful trance. I figured I needed to do something about the sails before the storm got too bad. I forced myself to get up and go outside. When I opened my door, the first person I saw was Ryker.

"Belle, I'm so sorry," he said desperately. "I was wrong…"

"I'm fine. Not everyone needs a boyfriend," I said curtly.

"Belle, please…"

"You're wasting time. Go tell the others there's a storm coming and then get to work," I ordered.

"If you would just listen…"

"There's nothing to listen to," I said, as I walked away. I began to climb into the rigging. I almost regretted being so rude to Ryker, but I couldn't help it. I didn't have any emotions left... not in my words or my mind. I soon reached the lowest spar and noticed that the rest of the crew had come to help, not that they were of any use. I began to work. It was easier now since it wasn't so cold, but a chill breeze stirred in the clouds. Rain began to fall from those dark clouds looming over the sky, acting as the tears I was too miserable to shed.

I had almost become immune to storms over the years. The wind and rain beating upon my shoulders had come to be an ordinary thing. I mindlessly untied the sail from the beam, unaware of anything around me. I acted as though my mind was simply somewhere else, but the truth was that my mind was nowhere at all. All reality had been lost, along with my wits and emotions. I didn't need to think to do my job. I didn't need to think at all. All thunderstorms were the same; that is… until I met this one.

I eventually climbed down from the sails and made my way to the steering wheel. I knew the waves would tip the *Pegasus* over if we didn't sail into them, but I was paying no attention to this at all. I turned around to see if all the sails were up... but everything went down from there. I suddenly caught a glimpse of Ryker's face. His eyes stared straight into mine; those dark, intense, sorrowful eyes that were an open window into his very soul. As I looked at him a flash of lightning within my miserable heart brought me back into reality. My mind and emotions all came back to me at once and my whole body trembled at the sight of that wistful glance. Tears began to stream down my cheeks, tears of misery and sorrow, tears of regret, and tears of rage.

I fell to my knees, in too much pain to even stand... that was only the beginning. The skies raged. The sea violently climbed high above the deck over and over, as though it would swallow us whole. I suddenly heard a terrible creaking sound. I was thrown down to one side of the deck as the waters came higher and higher. I found that I was lying against the rail and that the whole world had shifted. The *Pegasus* was capsizing.

For the shortest amount of time, I forced myself to think. The wind howled viciously as I tried to come up with a plan. I looked up at the sails. My eyes tried to avoid Ryker, but that was easy, once I saw that Sydney was *hoisting* the sails. Sydney had made it very clear that her brain was just *so* smart that it apparently skipped common sense, but now was a terrible time to prove it!

"*What are you doing?*" I shrieked.

"I don't have time to dumb it down for you, Belle. Just trust me!" Sydney yelled.

"That's not what you're supposed to do!" I screamed.

"Oh, sure! Everyone says, 'Sydney ruins everything. Sydney's so stupid'..."

"You *are* stupid!" I yelled.

"If we hoist the sails, the wind can keep the ship from capsizing. It's blowing the right way. It'll work, I promise. There! Are you happy? 'Cause I could go on and on..."

"Nope. That's good. You can stop now," I interrupted. I immediately ran to the highest mast and began to climb, blocking out any feeling or thought having to do with Ryker. I couldn't afford any distractions. I had to help my crew.

"Belle!" Ryker yelled. "Don't..."

"Leave me alone," I yelled.

"Don't mess with the highest sail. You..."

"I told you to leave me alone!" I cried.

"You'll get struck by lightning if you do!" Ryker screamed, but I didn't listen to him. I couldn't. His voice cut into my heart deeper than any knife, and his words burned through my soul more than any fire.

I continued my work, but there still weren't enough sails up for the wind to push the ship into an upright position. I tied down the lowest sail and began to move to the highest one. The ship violently swayed back and forth. I struggled to hold on to the ropes without falling into the tumultuous sea. It was even harder to hang on with a broken arm, but I had no other choice. It had come down to life or death.

"Belle! Get down from there!" Ryker screamed. "Please, I'm begging you!"

I blocked out his words and continued to climb.

"Belle! Belle, please, just listen to me! I know I hurt you, but I need you to listen to me!" Ryker begged.

"Shut up and leave me alone!" I pleaded.

"You could get struck by lightning if you go up there!" Ryker yelled.

"I told you to leave me alone!" I cried in anguish, tears streaming down my face. I reached the top of the highest sail and began to untie the ropes.

"Belle! Please! Listen to me!" Ryker shrieked.

I had made it very clear to him that I wasn't going to listen. Ryker saw that all his efforts had been in vain and, as I tried so desperately to avoid him, he did the most reckless, unexpected thing possible. *He jumped.*

He reached out his arms and caught the ropes just a few yards below me. I tried not to look at him. But then my eyes turned toward his, without my consent. He was pursuing me with every effort possible, but my heart had turned away from his love. As he came closer to me, I began to feel more and more pain.

"Don't you understand that every step you take toward me, every word you say, every look you give me cuts deeper and deeper into my soul?" I said coldly. "I don't care about the stupid lightning, and I'm not going to listen to you. Don't you get it? You're hurting me, just by looking at me! Please, just leave."

"I can't Belle," Ryker said, with the same intense passion in his eyes. "I know what I said earlier, but it wasn't true. I was wrong, and I'm sorry, I truly am. I know I hurt you, but I'm not perfect. No matter how hard I try, I can't be everything you need me to be. But please, please believe me when I say this: *I can't leave you.*"

All I could do was shake my head. Lightning flashed all around us. As I turned away from Ryker, I heard him say, "I'm sorry, I have to do this."

I suddenly felt his hand grasp the back of my shirt and pull me toward the sea. I screamed as I fell. The very second I grabbed hold of a rope to catch myself, a flash of light nearly blinded me as I heard a painful shriek, louder than the vicious thunder that accompanied all of this. I then saw that Ryker was falling, unconscious, into the sea. He'd been struck by lightning… in my place.

A storm began to rage in my broken heart; a storm more furious than the rain and wind surrounding me. I then came face-to-face with a terrifying realization that struck my heart much harder than any lightning could have: Ryker had just sacrificed his life for mine.

The same passionate love I'd always felt for him began to burn through my soul again, but it was only followed by horror. Ryker was about to die, and it was all my fault! *I* did this! *I* was in the wrong! Everything had been *my* fault!

Out of some unknown impulse shooting out from the depths of my heart, I plunged into the sea. The waves crashed over me as I struggled to swim. My broken arm throbbed in pain. I couldn't find my way to the surface again. My arm was too weak for me to swim. But I was not going to allow Ryker to die without at least trying to fix the wrong I'd done. If I died trying to save him, at least we'd die together.

With every wave that crashed down on me came more and more agony. I was beginning to lose my breath when I finally came to the surface. I gasped for air and helplessly cried, "Sydney! Sydney, help!"

"What is wrong with you?" Sydney shrieked.

"Sydney, please!" I screamed, as waves began to crash over me and pulled me under the water.

But just then, a spark of hope began to burn in my shattered heart as a flash of lightning struck the waters.

The sea was illuminated, and for just an instant I could see the cherished, yet heartbroken face I loved so much. I swam towards him and took hold of his arm. With the little strength I had left, I struggled to the surface.

My efforts were in vain. I could hardly swim or get anywhere. I had almost lost all hope and consciousness when I suddenly felt something hit me in the back of the head. I whirled backward and tried to feel around to find out what it was, but I was then seized by an unknown hand. When its ridiculously long fingernail dug into my arm, I realized it was Sydney.

I was brought to the surface and saw that Sydney had been holding a rope, so I grabbed it and pulled Ryker up with me.

"Belle! Belle? Did you grab the rope? Belle? Answer me! I can't see anything!" Sydney gasped.

"Your eyes are closed," I said faintly.

"Well, I know that, but…"

"Please, just get us back to the ship," I said.

"Yeah, come on," Sydney said, as she opened her eyes and blinked. When we made it back to the ship, she told me to take Ryker below deck and let the rest of the crew handle the ship.

I stayed down there for what seemed like an eternity. Tears relentlessly streamed down my cheeks as I held Ryker's motionless hand. A few hours had passed. He hadn't moved at all and I was beginning to worry. His back had been burned by the lightning and he was hardly breathing, but he *was* still alive. I didn't know whether he'd felt any pain, or simply felt nothing at all.

"I'm so sorry," I said dismally. "I should've listened to you. I just... you hurt me... so I... I just tried to block you out... but I should've forgiven you. Ryker, you're all I have left. I found all of my security in you, but I shouldn't have expected you to be perfect. But why, on Earth, would you want to give me away? I don't want Dylan, I want you. But I may have just lost you, and it was all my fault. You don't deserve to be in pain, I do. I'm so sorry any of this ever happened. But I'm not expecting you to give me another chance, since I didn't give you one. But I am now. I forgive you, and I'm hoping you forgive me. Because I can't leave you, either."

The silence after that was suddenly broken by my sadness. I hopelessly dug my face into my hands and sobbed. I heard footsteps and looked up. Sydney walked down the steps and sat next to me.

"If it makes you feel any better," she said, "only ten percent of people that get struck by lightning actually die."

"I don't know what that means," I sobbed.

"Well, you see, if one hundred people get struck by lightning…"

"Do you think I killed him?"

"That's what I'm getting to. There's only a ten percent chance…"

"Did I kill him or not?"

"Is he breathing?" Sydney asked.

I nodded.

"Then he'll probably be just fine," Sydney assured me. "You should probably get some rest. I bet you're pretty tired."

"No, I'm fine. I'd rather stay here," I said.

"Okay. The storm died down, so the rest of the crew will probably come down here soon," Sydney said as she got up to leave. "Don't worry. He'll be fine."

And so I remained with him. I wouldn't allow myself to sleep or go anywhere... not until I knew Ryker was okay.

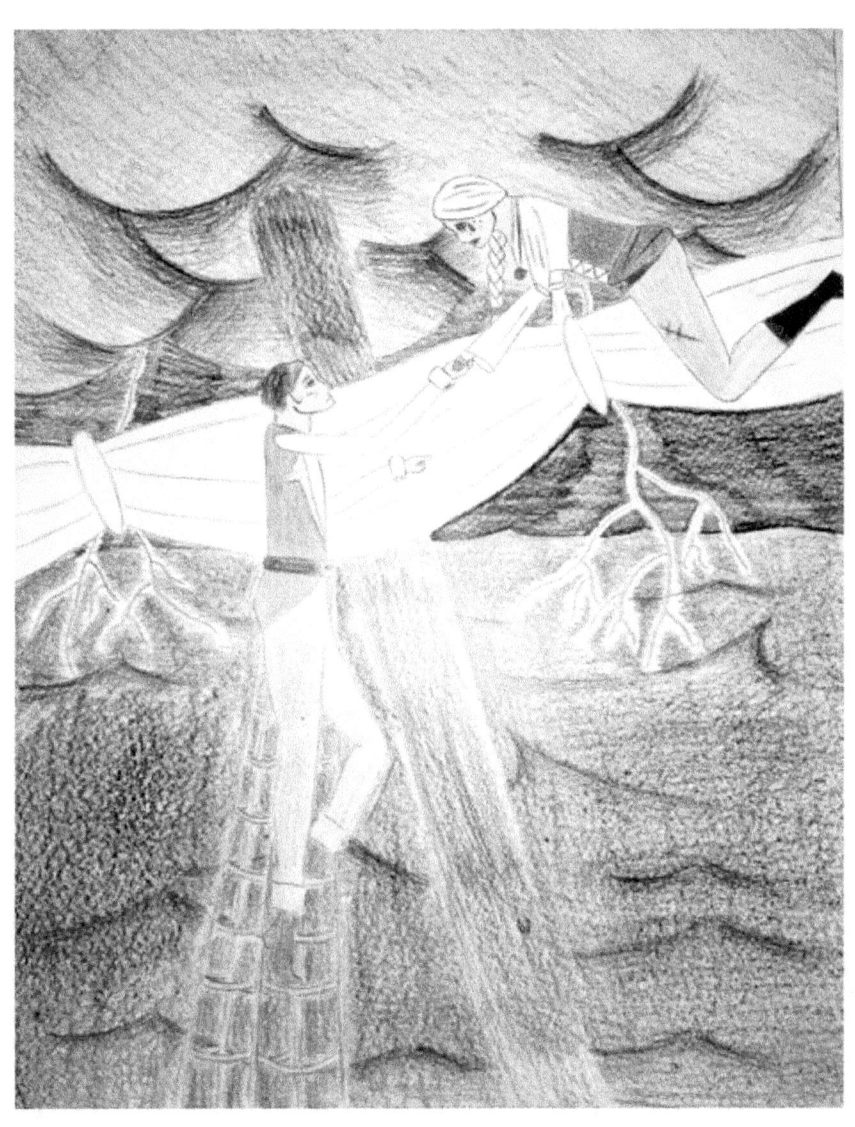

If I Die

The hours of the night slowly drifted away and morning came. I hadn't slept for a second. I was too worried to sleep or even be tired. I held Ryker's hand in mine and continuously prayed that he would wake up. Every second that went by without him made my heart ache more and more.

Then, as I miserably looked down at my hand, I saw that Ryker's fingers were wrapped around mine. Tears of joy burst from my eyes as I held Ryker up and kissed him.

"I'm so sorry," I sobbed pitifully. "I'm sorry you got struck by lightning, and I'm sorry I got mad at you, and I'm sorry I didn't listen to you, and I'll understand if you don't love me anymore because you almost died, and I know that you're probably really mad at me right now, and I'm not sure whether or not we broke up, but I wanna be your girlfriend again... if you can forgive me."

"I'll always forgive you. I love you. But I didn't catch hardly any of that," Ryker admitted.

"Wait... the lightning didn't, like, fry your brain, right? You remember who I am, right? Right?"

"I'm fine. The last thing I remember, I was struck by lightning."

I dug my face into Ryker's shoulder and sobbed. "I'm sorry. Everything is my fault. I'm so sorry. Can you please forgive me? Please?"

"I just did, remember?" Ryker said sweetly. "You don't have to go so hard on yourself. I have just as much to apologize for."

"No! Don't apologize! This is all my fault! I don't even deserve you..."

"Please, don't even get started with that. I love you, and I don't care whether or not you deserve me," Ryker said.

"I love you, too, I just…"

"What, you don't think I'm better off with Sydney, do you?" Ryker joked.

"Thanks for reminding me about that," I mumbled.

"Oh… I'm sorry… I didn't know you weren't over that yet," Ryker apologized. "Can I please explain? I know I'm in the wrong, but will you at least listen, please?"

"Why would you give me away?" I asked somberly.

"I don't want to give you away. Look… you know I'm… I don't know, insecure… about being wanted. I… I wanted you to have what was best for you. I thought that was Dylan…"

"You were wrong," I interrupted.

"Yes, I know that now. And I know I hurt you. And to be honest… I didn't want us to save him at first, but now I can see how selfish that was. I was afraid you'd want him, and that I'd be the one keeping you from him. I thought that I'd have to let you go. When I accepted the fact that we *would* save Dylan, I tried to accept the fact that I might lose you. I didn't want to fight over you like you were some possession, but at the same time, I did. I just wanted you to be happy."

"I'm happy with you," I told him.

"I know that... I just... You told me I was more than enough... and I don't think I can live up to that," Ryker admitted.

"You don't have to be enough, because, when it comes down to the cold hard truth, none of us ever will be. I shouldn't have expected you to be perfect... because you're not. And I'm not. None of us are."

"Do you remember, at the palace, when I told you I wouldn't let anyone take me from you? Well, I'm not gonna let Dylan take me from you either," Ryker promised.

"Oh, don't worry. Dylan hates me," I said.

"What do you mean? Did he hurt you?" Ryker asked defensively.

I stared at the ground. I couldn't tell him how much Dylan had hurt over the years. Ryker would kill him! But I couldn't lie to him. No, of course not!

"It's okay," Ryker said. "You don't have to tell me. We'll change the subject."

"Thanks," I said. "But you should probably get some rest."

"You're the one that needs rest. You're eyes are turning purple. You look like you haven't slept in forever."

"I couldn't. But I guess you're right, I'm pretty tired." I stood up and said, "I don't wanna just leave you here."

"I'll be fine," Ryker told me.

"You can hardly move," I argued. "What if you need something?"

"Then I'll make Sawyer get it for me. I don't mind ordering him around," Ryker said.

"Do you want me to get him for you?" I asked.

"I mean… if you want to."

"Sawyer!" I screamed. "Get your butt down here right now!"

"Hey, Ryker, guess what?" Sawyer yelled as he kicked open the door.

"Oh no," Ryker sighed.

"I was useful last night!" Sawyer exclaimed.

Ryker rolled his eyes. I was sure he'd be fine, so I went to my room and crashed into my hammock. I slept well for a while, but when I woke up my arm was beginning to hurt again. I wondered if I'd be able to fight Clark with my arm the way it was.

I thought to myself, "Maybe it'll heal before we get there. When will we get there, anyway? It's supposed to only be a two-week voyage… that's fourteen days… we're on day eleven. So that gives us… tomorrow is twelve… then thirteen… then on day fourteen we arrive… so counting today, that's… eleven, twelve, thirteen… three more days. Three days! That's not enough time at all! My arm won't work, Ryker's crippled, and half the crew can't fight. I'm not ready!

No, I'm not ready at all! I'm gonna get myself killed out there.

"What if I die? No, I can't die. I can't just leave the crew behind. But if I die, won't it be worth it, for Dylan's sake? No! No, I can't leave Ryker. It'll break his heart. But it's not Ryker's heart I'm worried about. I'm worried about Dylan's life. No, of course, I'm worried about Ryker. But what if I can escape Clark? I have to! I can't die."

I got up, grabbed my sword, and began to sharpen it. I had to fight back. Either that, or I'd have to choose between Ryker and Dylan. I'd obviously choose Ryker. No. If I didn't die, Dylan would. But I didn't want to die! I hated the thought of being slaughtered the way my parents were. I hated Clark. I hated him with every bone in my body. But I feared him even more than I hated him. I hadn't feared him before, but it had finally dawned on me that he was going to kill me! He had no use for me anymore!

In three days, I would walk straight into death... willingly. No! No, I couldn't do that! But I had to! I had no idea what I was going to do, but I did know one thing. Clark Teach was my sworn enemy from that day forward.

I could hear footsteps coming across the deck. I furiously sharpened my sword. And just as my door opened, I saw my enemy's face staring straight at me! Filled with a burning and uncontrollable rage, I threw my sword at him and screamed, "Get out! Get out! I hate you! Get away from me!"

I then heard a pathetic British voice shriek, "Why are all the girls on this ship trying to kill me? Sydney, you're friend is absolutely delusional!"

I looked up and saw *Michael* standing in my doorway. I was so shocked that I lost my balance and fell against the wall. I just stared at him, too traumatized to even speak.

"Sydney wanted me to check on you," Michael said timidly. "She says you might be mentally unstable since you almost killed Ryker last night. She said that the last time that happened, you started having conversations with yourself. Well, are you just going to stand there? Can you please tell me why you threw a sword at me? Is it because I'm rich? Because it's really not my fault…"

I shook my head.

"Do you need something?" he asked. "I'm starting to worry. You seem to have a lack of sanity."

"That's probably because I'm going to die soon and there's nothing I can do about it!" I cried.

"I don't think this has anything to do with me, does it?" Michael asked.

"I'm going to die," I said to myself.

"Well, you're acting very strange. I'll let you get back to whatever you were doing," Michael said, as he left.

I remained in my room for a few minutes, still fearing for my life. I had no idea what to do with my fate.

After a while, I figured there was work to be done, so I got up and went outside. The sunlight shimmered on the quiet sea as the pink clouds peacefully rolled across the sky (it was the only form of pink I would tolerate). A few dolphins leaped across the rippling waters happily. The soft wind blew through my hair and gave me a small sense of joy.

The sea had always given me some sort of unexplainable hope. Its endlessness brought endless peace. Its magnificence stretched beyond the horizon. I had never really understood why it had given me such hope, but I now I was beginning to understand... maybe. Perhaps, if the One who had created so majestic a sea had also created me, then maybe He also controlled my fate just as He controlled the shimmering waters. Not in the sense that He controlled *me*. No, I had free will. But He controlled everything around me.

Then it made me wonder. If God controlled everything around me, then hadn't He intended for me to be at the ball that night? Hadn't He intended for the palace to be robbed? Hadn't He intended for me to set out on this voyage? And if He had, then shouldn't I choose to go along with it?

My job was easy. God had already sent the winds to the place He wanted me to go. All I had to do was hoist my sails. If God wanted me to live, then He'd let me live. If not, then I'd die an honorable death. The idea was simple.

"Belle! Stop trying to kill my boyfriend! What is wrong with you?" Sydney shrieked, running up onto the deck.

"I didn't..."

"You know, twenty percent..."

"I don't know what stupid percent is, Sydney!" I
interrupted.

"Just because I'm smart, doesn't mean I'm nerdy!"
Sydney said defensively.

"I didn't say..."

"Ryker said! Yes! Your boyfriend insulted me! I am
offended, Belle! Offended!" Sydney screamed.

"I'm on team Ryker," I said blatantly.

"I was here first!" Sydney jumped up and down
angrily.

"You're the one who kissed him," I said placidly.

"You've kissed him a gazillion times!" Sydney spat.
"And that's a lot, because a gazillion's not even a
number!"

"It's not?" I gasped.

"Enough of your sarcasm! Enough!" Sydney shrieked.

"You always said it as though it were a number. I just..."

"No!"

"But then, which numbers are real? No, like actually. I never went to school. I still use my fingers to count. I was raised in a cargo hold," I admitted.

"I know! You've told us a hundred times!" Sydney screamed

"A hundred's not a number!" I yelled.

"Why are we even fighting over this?" Sydney asked furiously.

"Because I threw a sword at your boyfriend!" I screamed.

"Do you *want* me to slap you?" Sydney yelled.

"I thought he was Clark!"

"How?" Sydney shrieked.

"I don't know," I told her, breaking down in tears.

"Um… can we like… stop fighting now… because I'd hug you… but we're fighting," Sydney said awkwardly.

"Why does everything always happen to me?" I sobbed.

"I don't how to respond to that," Sydney replied.

"I just… I don't… I don't wanna die… and I… I know it's selfish…"

"I mean, you're a Christian, so you'll live either way," Sydney said, trying to comfort me.

"But Ryker needs me… and I… I can't leave him," I said in tears.

"I don't understand," Sydney said.

"Why don't you know how to have a conversation?" I cried.

"Because I'm socially awkward!" Sydney answered. "Well, I'm glad I don't cry as much as you do, because I have allergies and then I can't breathe. You know, you should probably cheer up for medical reasons. You don't wanna get pneumonia or something like that."

"You're the one who decided to room with a rat!" I yelled.

"Ferret! Gerald Templeton is a ferret!" Sydney screamed.

"I don't care!"

Sydney stared at me in silence. Maybe she'd just run out of things to argue about. All I could hear was the sea now as more tears continued to roll down my face.

"So... why did you throw a sword at Michael?" Sydney asked calmly.

"I don't know," I sighed. "I was... I was thinking about Clark... and then I saw Michael... and I was just... I was scared and it was my first reaction."

"Because he startled you?" Sydney asked.

"Sydney, I know I sound crazy, but I *did* see Clark," I assured her.

"Maybe you were hallucinating... but you didn't mean to hurt *Michael*, right?"

I shook my head.

"Well, you should've just said that. I forgive you," Sydney told me. "But if you're so upset about confronting Clark, why don't we just turn back?"

"Because Clark has just about killed Dylan and I can't take it anymore. I have to do this. I'm perfectly capable, and I if don't, then I may as well just join the other side."

"But what if you're not capable?" Sydney asked worriedly.

"Then I'll fight as hard as I can, until I can't anymore," I replied.

"But aren't afraid of, well... dying?"

"Of course I'm afraid. I'm afraid of death, and pain, and anything else that might happen. But my passion's greater than my fear and I'll do whatever I can until there's nothing left," I decided.

"I don't understand how anyone could have that kind of courage," Sydney admitted. "I mean, every now and then I'll do something brave 'cause I'm just not thinking at the time, but I'm usually the one to chicken out."

"We can't chicken out. Not this time," I said. I didn't know if it was for Sydney, or for me.

I suddenly heard rapid footsteps coming onto the deck. I turned around and saw Sawyer, Ginger, and Alice clumsily climbing onto the deck.

"Did you know that chickens can run around with their heads cut off?" Sawyer exclaimed.

"We're trying to have a conversation. Go away," Sydney whined.

"Sydney, are you a skirt-roller?" Alice asked.

"Are *you* a skirt-roller?" Sydney returned.

"What's a skirt-roller?" Ginger asked.

"Someone who rolls the top of their skirt over and over to make it shorter," Sydney answered. "Now, can you please go?"

"It's November, and we can see your thighs," Alice pointed out. "Belle, you should make her walk the plank."

"No one's walking the plank. Now go," I said.

"Come on. Leave Belle alone," Sydney said, as she guided those small annoying kids below deck.

The salty breeze continued to blow through my hair as the sea stretched into the orange sunset. I took a deep breath as the last light faded away. Then the last trace of sunlight vanished, and I made my final resolution to rescue Dylan no matter the cost.

Don't Look Back

We were now on day thirteen of our voyage. I decided to have everyone meet that morning to try to prepare for the upcoming fight. Ryker was able to walk again, which made me feel a little less worried. My arm was beginning to feel better, too. However, I still felt as though our crew wasn't ready.

"So, where does this pirate hide most of his stolen jewels?" Michael asked.

"Um... he'll usually store it in caves that he can fit the *Cobra* into," I answered. "So, in this case, somewhere in Crossbone Cove. His ship can't hold it all, but he usually keeps his most valuable treasures in a storage room below deck. Check there first."

"Oh, kinda like your gold hoard that goes up to the *ceiling*?" Sydney retorted.

"You have stolen gold, too?" Michael exclaimed.

"I didn't steal it, I found it. It was just buried on some island for anyone to take," I said. "But anyway, Michael, I want you to go find the jewels and take them back to our ship. Don't try to fight anyone unless you really have to. Just get in and get out. Ryker, I need you to go with me to find Dylan. Clark's gonna try to keep him, not the jewels, if he has to make a choice. Dylan's practically his slave, so I don't want to be alone if something were to happen. The rest of you, just be there when you're needed and fight when you have to. Ginger, stay with your brother so you two can protect each other."

"You're not gonna make us hide, like last time?" Alice asked.

"No, not this time," I replied.

"*Squawk!* What about me?" Donna inquired.

"Oh, right... *you,*" I scoffed. "Um... I don't care... just don't be annoying."

"I am beginning to get the feeling I'm not needed. *Squawk!* Explain yourself!" Donna demanded.

"Well… you're not very useful," I admitted.

"What?" Donna screeched. "Oh, so am I just not human enough to be a part of this crew? *Squawk!* I could peck every one of those pirates' eyes out."

"That's really not necessary," I tried to tell her.

"Oh, but saving your ex-husband is necessary! Sure! *Squawk!* You do that! I'll just stay here! Alone! Useless! *Squawk!* And let me tell you something about your current husband! He treats me like a football! That's what I said! *Squawk!* A *football!*"

"I don't even know what a football is!" Ryker exclaimed.

"It's probably some oddly shaped ball that boys tackle each other for, to throw and run around with. Sounds very twentieth-century," Sydney guessed.

"*Squawk!* I'm not an oddly shaped ball! But I *was* thrown! And I hit the ground very hard!" Donna griped.

"But you can fly," Ginger pointed out.

"*Squawk!* My brain is small! I can't remember things like that!" Donna yelled.

"So," Ryker started," You admit that your brain..."

"Shut up! Just shut up!" Donna squawked as she flew below deck in a fit. We all stared as she left and then went back to our conversation.

"Well, that's that," I announced. "Questions?"

"What if... I don't... I..." Ginger stammered. "I don't... I'm scared."

"I know you're scared. We all are," I told her. "But we need all the help we can get. You can go with Michael if you want. He'll need an extra hand. Alice, look after Sawyer."

"What?" Sawyer protested. "I don't need looking after! I'm a man!"

"No, you're not. Sit down," Ryker said.

"Prove it!" Sawyer demanded.

"You're four-foot-three with no muscle and a high-pitched voice," Ryker said blatantly.

"At least I'm not as short as Sydney!" Sawyer yelled.

"Sydney ran up and down the deck screaming about how she'd finally hit five feet, just a few months ago," I corrected him.

"Well, Michael's short, too!" Sawyer went on.

"Five-foot-two is not short!" Michael exclaimed.

"Yes, it is!" Ryker laughed.

"Don't talk to my boyfriend that way!" Sydney griped.

"Okay, okay, Michael's not *that* short..." Alice started. "Compared to Sydney's skirt."

"Oh, really? There's worse out there!" Sydney yelled.

"Everybody sit down and be quiet!" I ordered. So they all sat down and stopped arguing, for once. I took a deep breath and said, "There's one more thing I have to tell you. If I… if I don't make it… I want Ryker to take my place."

"No," Ryker objected. "No, you'll make it, won't you?"

"I… I don't know," I answered, my voice shaking. "Can we… can we talk about this… later?"

"Yeah… sure," Ryker said nervously. "Later."

Not long after, the rest of the crew left. Ryker and I stayed. We just stared at each other, broken-hearted, until I finally began to cry. Ryker came to comfort me, but it was of no use.

"I'm sorry," I sobbed. "I don't want to have to leave you. I just… I can't let Dylan be tortured to death. He's not more important than you, and I'm not choosing him over you, but it's a matter of life and death, and I… I have to save him… I need you to understand that."

"I understand… and I'm not trying to keep you from saving him," Ryker said gently. "I didn't know it was this serious. I'm not sure what I can do, but I'll give you whatever you need."

"I need you to survive," I pleaded. "You have to be here to take care of the others. I don't want you to try and sacrifice yourself for me. It would hurt me too much to see you die."

"But what about you? I can't just let you die," Ryker said.

"I know… and I'm sorry… I really am!" I cried. "I know I'm hurting you… and that you don't want me to go… but you have to be strong… for me. I can't live without you. You have to survive. Maybe we can both make it out alive. Maybe not."

"Maybe we will," Ryker assured me as he wistfully looked into my eyes.

"You look like you're about to cry," I said sadly.

"I haven't cried in ten years, I don't even think I can anymore," Ryker admitted. "But if I could cry, I would."

"I wish none of this had ever happened," I sighed.

"We all do," Ryker said. I looked up at him with sorrow and hopelessness. I felt as though I were telling him 'goodbye' now since it would be too painful later. Unable to even look at Ryker, I closed my eyes, dug my face into his shoulder, and continued to cry.

The hours of that afternoon and night passed by slowly, filled with anxiety and fear. Then the day came which I had dreaded with every bone in my body. I had made up my mind. I would fight for a noble cause and die an honorable death. I was almost so afraid that I wanted to turn back, but that was no longer possible. We had arrived at Crossbone Cove.

Mist sealed the entrance of the wretched cave. As we crept through, everyone remained silent at the front of the *Pegasus*. My heart beat rapidly. My whole body was shaking and I felt sick. But I had no time for fear or doubt. I had no time to look back. And as the mist rolled back I saw that massive wooden cobra carved into the stern of its deadly ship. We inched closer and closer.

I prayed one last time that I might make it out alive, and then, my voice shaking, I yelled, *"Attack!"*

Keep Fighting

The Stowaways leaped onto the *Cobra* with valor in place of fear.

Blood was already beginning to spill across the deck. There was no sign of Clark, only his murderous crew of pirates. I fought my way through the bloodthirsty men until I came to the hatch leading below deck.

I suddenly felt a hand grip my shoulder. I quickly spun around and saw a vicious pirate with brutal intentions. Before he could do anything, I punched him in the throat and sliced his arm with my sword. I noticed that Ryker was close by, so I had to beat this man soon. I brought up my leg and kicked his neck. The pirate fell to the ground.

I managed to open the hatch as Ryker ran toward me. Before anyone else could notice, we had begun to climb into the cargo hold.

"Should we have stayed to help them?" Ryker asked quietly.

"They're fine. We have to save our energy. Come on," I ordered. "Clark's probably waiting for us right now. Keep going down. I'll tell you when to stop."

Our surroundings grew darker and darker until I finally told Ryker we were on the right level. As I stepped onto the floor, I realized that I was shaking. Ryker put his hand on my shoulder to try and comfort me. I looked at him and he nodded.

"Go on. Fight me," I yelled into the darkness. "But I won't stop on until I can either free Dylan or die in the process."

There was no answer. I caught sight of a faint light in the back of the room and began to walk toward it. Ryker followed close behind.

"I know you've been waiting for me. I know you think of this as a trap. You think you've bested me!" I shouted. "You haven't bested me until we fight!"

Again there was no answer. I turned around. No one was there, save Ryker. I looked all around me. Clark wasn't there.

"Something's wrong," I whispered as I continued to walk. "Clark's waiting to kill me, I just know it. Why wouldn't he be here?"

"He might not know you're trying to free Dylan," Ryker guessed.

"No. He's smarter than you think. He found out somehow," I said.

I kept walking and called, "Dylan? Dylan, are you there?"

Then I heard a faint voice coming out from the darkness that made my heart jump.

"*Belle?*"

Tears formed in my eyes as I ran toward Dylan. When I finally saw him, I wrapped my arms around him and cried. Being without him had been like being without the only family member I ever had. The night I sailed away from that wretched place, I was so sure I'd never see him again.

"You… you came back for me?" Dylan asked.

"Always," I said softly. It broke my heart to see all that was left of Dylan was skin and bones with one eye and one hand. His hand was cuffed and chained to the wall and he looked like he'd just been whipped.

"We're gonna get you out of here as soon as we can, okay?" I told Dylan, though I had no idea how.

Meanwhile, Michael and Ginger had begun to make their way to the storage room. Michael peeked through a hole in the door and said, "There's no one in there. It's safe to go in."

"You're sure?" Ginger asked timidly.

"Positive," Michael assured her. The door opened easily as they entered a room filled with stolen treasures. There, in the center, stood the Queen of England's jewels. Clark hadn't even tried to hide them.

"You can grab the necklaces and bracelets. I'll get the rest," Michael said as he picked up a tiara. He continued to rummage through the treasures until he suddenly heard a helpless scream. Michael whirled around to see Ginger lying unconscious on the floor.

"Did you really think it'd be that easy?" A sly voice asked.

Michael looked up and stared into the malicious eyes of Clark Teach himself. He just stared, shocked and confused. He stumbled backward and gasped, "*I… I know you.*"

Back in the cargo hold, I anxiously paced back and forth, trying to come up with a plan.

"Belle, you really don't have to do this," Dylan insisted.

"If I don't free you, you'll die," I argued.

"Well, you're just getting all worked up over nothing," Dylan said.

"Is there a key somewhere?" Ryker asked.

"It's probably in Clark's cabin. Don't go in there. Never go in there," Dylan told us.

"You know where to find me," I said as I took off running for the ladder. I climbed and climbed and eventually reached the deck. I fought through the crowd and made it to the cabin. The door was locked. I threw my pistol at the window and the glass broke. I reached inside, unlocked the door, and opened it. I began to rummage through all of the chests, but there was no sign of the key.

I looked around me and suddenly came face-to-face with the biggest pirate I had ever seen. Before I could help myself, he grabbed my neck and said, "Clark said you was quite the troublemaker. Well, we can end that real quick. He wants you... alive and in one piece. I could kill you right now if I wanted to. You're lucky."

"You could if... if you didn't... didn't waste so much time... talking," I stammered, unable to breathe. I raised my gun to his arm and threatened, "If you don't let me go... I'll shoot."

"Nice try." The pirate took one hand off my neck to grab my gun. I freed myself and hit him as hard as I could on the head with my gun. He stumbled. I hit him again and he fell to the ground. Then, I continued my search for the key.

In the storage room, Michael was still staring at Clark. All of the color had drained from his face. He was baffled beyond imagination, and he had no idea why.

"Of course you know me," Clark scoffed.

"But I... I've never even met you," Michael said.

"You have," Clark snarled. "Does this day sound familiar to you? January 18th, 1680?"

"The... the day I was born," Michael said.

"And it should have been the day you died!" Clark yelled as he punched Michael. "You're weak, you know that?"

"How do you know anything about me?" Michael cried.

"Because," Clark stepped closer and pushed his sword against Michael's neck. "*You're my son.*"

I had turned Clark's cabin upside-down. The key wasn't there. I hurried back to Ryker and Dylan and quickly said, "The key's not in there."

"Then just chop my other hand off, or something," Dylan said. "At least I'll make it out alive."

"Where's the storage room?" Ryker asked.

"Up one more level on the right," I answered.

"I'll go check there," Ryker said as he hurried away. "You need a break."

Ryker disappeared into the darkness. I leaned against the wall and held my arm to stop it from bleeding.

"You shouldn't have gone out there again. Your arm's drenched in blood. I told you not to go. You're the one who didn't listen," Dylan scoffed.

"Do you want me to get you out of here, or not?" I snapped. "Is there any cloth in here?"

"It's over there," Dylan told me. I picked up the cloth and began to bandage my arm with it.

Unable to wait for Ryker, I told Dylan I was going to help him and hurried into the void of darkness.

Meanwhile, tears streamed down Michael's helpless face as he timidly said, "That's impossible."

"You didn't think I was going to kill you before explaining your defeat, did you?" Clark scoffed. "See, when you were born, your pathetic mother hid you from me, to protect your worthless little life. She eventually ran away to England and married Phillip Evans. Over the years, I gathered news of you and your family and noticed your loyalty to England. I realized that if I stole the queen's jewels, you'd be the only one foolish enough to walk right into my trap. And here you are."

"You're going to kill me?" Michael stammered.

"Yes," Clark said as he tightly held Michael's neck in front of his sword.

At that very instant, Michael freed himself from Clark's grip and drew his sword.

"Don't make me fight you!" Michael cried. "I never did anything to harm you. I don't understand how you could possibly be so heartless as to kill your own son!"

"Of course, you don't understand!" Clark laughed. "You've been sheltered from evil your whole life. And now that you have to fight, you don't even know your opponent."

Michael, overcome with shock, swung his sword into Clark's arm and cut it. Clark punched Michael and he fell to the ground. He drew closer and closer to Michael, pointed his gun to Michael's head, and…

"*Let him go!*" a voice cried, just before Clark yelled in pain and dropped his gun. He whirled around and there stood Ryker.

"I see that scar never healed," Clark said as he maliciously stared into Ryker's eyes. Michael took Ginger and ran away, as Ryker made the first blow. A gruesome fight broke out between them. The floor became drenched in blood. Fury devoured both hearts as the cling of swords filled the room.

I anxiously climbed through the darkness and caught sight of the storage room. The sounds of pain and hatred made my heart stop. I found myself unable to move, paralyzed by fear.

"So this is it," I thought. "When I go in there, he'll kill me. But I have to go in. If rescuing Dylan and Ryker requires a fight, I can't turn that fight down. Then why don't I just go? Because I'm afraid. Well, that's stupid. Just go. No, I can't. Why not? Because I'm afraid. But Clark will never stop this madness unless I fight him. He'll kill Ryker and he'll keep torturing Dylan if I don't do something. I'm the one he wants. Either I'll defeat him, or he'll defeat me and finally be satisfied. This trap was set for me. The only way to end it is to walk into it."

My fear was the only thing holding me down. I was my own obstacle. I then realized that I didn't have to be afraid of anything at all. All I had to do was fight for justice. After all, I served the God of justice, not fear. So, if I was wrapped in chains of fear, the only thing I had to do to break them was to have courage.

I rushed to the storage room. My heart beat rapidly. My hands shook. But I was no longer afraid. Not anymore. I stood in front of the room and stopped.

"You wanted to fight me, didn't you?" I said boldly.

The fighting between Clark and Ryker stopped. All fell silent. Ryker tried to stop Clark as he stepped closer to me.

"Ryker, stop," I ordered. "You have other things to do."

"Belle, please, let me help you," Ryker pleaded.

"You've done enough," Clark growled. He swung his sword at Ryker's head. I stopped his blade with my own.

"I'm not afraid of you. Go on. Fight me," I taunted.

"If that's what you wish," Clark said slyly. *The fight had come.*

Our swords crashed into each other over and over. As we fought, Ryker slipped past us with the key and an uneasy look in his eyes. Before long, I was drenched in blood and sweat. But I kept fighting, and I wouldn't give up until I knew Dylan was free. I had to keep Clark here, away from Dylan, until then.

I suddenly felt a searing pain in my hand, but I didn't dare to look down for even a second. I gripped my hand in pain and stumbled onto the wall.

"You wanted to fight," Clark laughed. "Are you satisfied now?"

"One day, you'll lose," I panted. "Then I'll be satisfied."

"Why don't you just kill me now?" Clark asked.

"Because you're the monster, not me," I grunted.

Rage filled Clark's terrible eyes. As he tried to punch me, I cut his arm with my sword. Blood spewed out of his veins, but his fury was unrelenting. We fought for what seemed like forever. The clash of our swords was music to his ears; it was torture to mine.

Clark flung his sword into my left arm and grabbed my blade. He crossed the two in front of my neck and said, "I'm not going to kill you. I would never waste a perfectly good *slave*."

That word echoed through my ears and made my heart drop into my stomach. All this time, he hadn't been wanting to kill me. He wanted to use me. For evil.

"As long as I live, I will *never* work for you, ever again!" I cried as I took back my sword and jabbed it into Clark's shoulder. His blade had cut deep into my arm, but I had to ignore that. I swung my sword across his side and blocked his. We continued to fight, drawing blood every few moments.

After a while, I began to feel lightheaded. I was exhausted and soaked in blood. This could not be happening. I stopped to breathe just for a split second. I shouldn't have let my guard down. Within that split second, Clark punched me and I fell to the ground. My head was spinning. I could hardly see. I didn't even have the strength to stand up.

"You're a fool," Clark scoffed. "Did you really think you could win? No, of course not. When I heard you'd be at that stupid palace, I purposefully broke in that night. I let Dylan leave his little note. He was the bait. I let him tell you all of the terrible things I've done on purpose, just to give you more reasons to hate me. I lured you in. You came willingly. You were blind. And now, here you are. My slave. Defeated."

"You haven't defeated me yet," I said. "I knew this was a trap. I knew you were waiting for me. I'm no fool. I simply wanted justice more than my own life."

"Is that so?" Clark said as he grabbed my arm. He suddenly threw me against the wall and everything went black.

When I woke up, it was still pitch-black and silent aside from the monotonous sound of water dripping from the ceiling. I realized I was in the brig.

"Belle?" a voice asked.

A spark of hope burned in my soul as I called into the darkness, "Ryker?"

I then saw him carrying a dim lantern. He walked toward the iron bars and lovingly reached for my hand.

"Dylan's safe. He's on the *Pegasus*. I'm gonna get you out of here," Ryker whispered. "Can you walk?"

"Yeah."

"Stand back," Ryker said. He put his gun in the keyhole and pulled the trigger. The bullet flew through the lock and into a bundle of cloth. The lock was blown to pieces. Ryker opened the door and helped me up.

"Clark wants me as his slave. We have to go. Now," I demanded, as I got up and stumbled.

"You okay?" Ryker asked. "You're bleeding. A lot."

"Yeah… I'm fine," I answered.

We started to leave but then saw a light coming from the ladder. My heart stopped.

"Ah, you're just who I wanted." Clark came down the stairs with Michael, whose hands were tied together. Clark threw Michael onto the floor and grabbed Ryker.

"Get away from him!" I screamed as I cut off Clark's arm. "Kill me instead!" I begged. "Please! Please, just let him go! Let him go!"

Clark pressed his sword to Ryker's throat and said nothing.

"Belle, just take Michael and go," Ryker pleaded.

"If you would just surrender, I'd let him go. Or, you could leave right now: your life in one piece, perfectly free. But I'll kill him," Clark said.

"Belle, just go," Ryker pleaded.

I would never, ever leave Ryker to die. But I could also never surrender. I would do what I'd planned to do... fight.

"I'll stay," I decided. "Let him go."

"Don't get any ideas," Clark grunted. Just before he let Ryker go, he stabbed him, but not enough to kill him.

"You said you'd let him go!" I cried.

"Of course. You wouldn't be staying otherwise," Clark said.

"Belle, you don't have to do this," Ryker urged.

I held his hand in mine and quietly said, "Ryker, I'd rather you and Michael escape than for me to live in freedom. You have to get out of here. Do it for me."

"I'll come back for you," Ryker promised.

"Don't. Just get the crew to safety and go," I said.

"Why not?"

"Because there might not be anyone left to come back for," I said, as tears began to run down my cheeks. "I'll keep him busy while you get Michael."

"I should be the one that has to die," Ryker pleaded. "You never deserved this."

"I'm not afraid of death," I shook my head," Just go."

"I can't."

"Please. You have to... for my sake."

"Get on with it," Clark grunted, as he took me away.

"Let her go!" Ryker screamed. "Please! Please take me instead!"

"Ryker, you can't do this to me!" I yelled.

"I can't just let him torture you to death!" Ryker cried.

"You have to," I begged. Ryker looked at me as though he were trying to fight back tears. But he didn't cry. He couldn't cry.

"I love you," Ryker said, as he let go of my hand, possibly for the last time.

"I love you, too," I said. I turned toward Clark with sorrow. He forced me back to the jail cell, but as I reached the door, I stopped.

"Get in the cell!" Clark yelled as he slapped my face.

"No."

"Now!" Clark thundered.

"No," I replied. "Not as long as I live will I ever obey you, or submit to you. Never."

"Well," Clark grinned. "That means the boy dies."

I punched Clark in the throat. I would never let Ryker die.

"I told you I'd stay, and you let him go," I shouted. "And I will stay. I'll stay here, dead and in pieces, in this brig forever. But I will never bow to you, and I will never work for you, Clark! Terror may be your greatest weapon, but I'm not afraid to fight you to the death! And the only way you'll ever take my freedom is by prying it from my cold dead fingers, and even then my soul would have left this world and you would have lost!"

I suddenly thrust my sword into Clark's face and took out one of his eyes. He fought back. We went on thrashing our swords at each other, drawing more and more blood every second. Clark then cut off part of my shoulder and I wailed in pain.

"You know anyone who's no use to me is dead," Clark snarled.

"Fine, then," I said coldly. I plunged my sword into Clark's chest, but not deep enough. In his rage, he punched me and swung his blade across my arm. He then picked up a whip and I froze.

Every memory of the pain caused by that whip flooded back into my mind. Memories that went all the way back to my youngest years and could never fade away. I had tried to forget, but it had always been impossible. I suddenly found myself reliving those memories, as Clark whipped me over and over, as I screamed in anguish.

He had caused too much agony, too many deaths, and too much heartbreak, and I had had enough. I grabbed the whip with my bare hands and began to violently thrash it at Clark. He stole the whip from my hands and threw it onto the ground. Then, he grabbed my shirt and maliciously yelled, "You've lost, Smith! I killed your parents, and now it's time for me to kill you. You were stupid to think you could defeat a man like me. You've lost."

"No. You're the one that lost," I said, my voice cold and filled with anger. "You lost the day you committed your life to evil. And unless you change, you'll always be defeated."

"You think I'm a monster," Clark spat on the ground. "You're weak."

"No, I'm not. As long as I'm fighting for the right cause, I'll always be strong... stronger than you, even," I declared, fighting my pain. "Mark my words, Clark. The prideful will fall, the hateful will be hated, and monsters like you will eventually become their own victims. Then, the only person you've defeated is yourself."

"We'll see about that," Clark scoffed. I was now pinned to the wall. I was in so much pain, I could hardly even fight back.

But then, before I could escape, before I could save myself, Clark pressed his pistol to my heart and grinned with the rotten teeth. He fired. The loud *bang* was drowned out by my screaming. I clutched my chest in agony, but I wasn't going to let Clark win. No, I couldn't. Just before I fell to the ground, I stooped down, hurled my sword at Clark one last time, and cut off his leg.

I ran into the darkness that surrounded us to hide myself. Just as I slipped out of sight, my whole body gave way and I collapsed. I was still conscious, but hardly even alive. I stayed there, motionless, waiting for my death.

Worth Crying Over

The only thing I could feel was anguish. I was in so much pain and so weak that I couldn't even move. I was struggling to breathe. I was drenched in blood. The only thing left for me was death.

In those terrible moments, I thought of the crew, of how I'd have to leave them, and of the fact that they didn't want this to happen, either. But at least they were safe. That was all that mattered. They were safe.

But they were heartbroken. They had all adored me, and half the time I didn't even know why. *Ryker* had adored me. Tears came to my eyes as I thought of him. He had loved everything about me. He'd tried so hard to give his life for mine. I knew I'd hurt him, but I had to hurt him to save him, and I hated myself for it.

I felt like I'd torn my very soul in half. But I couldn't have let Ryker die. I was the one that brought him into this, it was my fight. And now he couldn't get out of my mind. I saw his face over and over and cried more and more every time. I wanted to say 'goodbye' to him. I prayed that I would, but my hopes were low.

His voice was ringing in my ears, like a song I'd loved from the depths of my heart. I couldn't stop thinking about Ryker. I saw his eyes that were so deep they could shatter my heart. I felt his hands in mine. I heard his voice, even louder this time.

"Belle."

I was sure I was hallucinating and said nothing.

"Please. If you're alive, say something. Please. I need to know if you're alive."

I wanted to turn over to see if he was really there, but I couldn't. I tried to say his name, but my voice hardly even worked.

"Ryker?"

I suddenly saw a dim light shining on the wall. Ryker had come back for me. I began to cry even more as I realized he was there.

"I'm so sorry," I sobbed.

"No, no. It's okay. You'll be okay," Ryker said gently, as he picked me up and held me in his arms.

"No, I won't," I said, as tears streamed down my face.

"No, I'm gonna get you out of here, and then you'll be okay." Ryker brushed my hair away from my face. "I came back, just like I promised."

"You have to go," I insisted.

"Not without you."

"There's no use in… taking me with you."

"You'll die if I don't take you with me," Ryker argued.

"I'll die… either way," I told him.

"No… No, you don't really mean that," Ryker stared at me in shock. "No… you… you're just… you're exaggerating. That's all. You'll be okay."

"He shot my heart," I stammered. "It's too late for you to save me. I'm sorry."

"I'll bandage it with something, and..."

"Ryker," I stopped him. "Denial isn't gonna do you any good. I know you don't want me to leave, but I don't have a choice. *I'm dying.*"

Ryker's eyes stared into mine with so much sorrow that it made my very soul weep. I could see his anguish. I watched as his heart split in two. I watched as his soul throbbed in pain the way mine had back at Lost Island, the day he'd given his life for the crew... for me. And now I had to do the same, and it hurt far worse than the bullet in my chest.

Ryker tried desperately to fight his tears. I may have felt terrible then, but my heart screamed in anguish when two tears ran down Ryker's cheeks... the first he'd shed in ten years.

"I never meant to hurt you. I'm so sorry," I sobbed. "I'm so sorry."

"No, it's not your fault," Ryker said.

"You're crying."

"You're worth crying over," Ryker told me, as he wiped away my tears.

"You shouldn't have to cry over me."

Ryker said nothing.

"Is there something you need to tell me?" I asked, struggling to breathe.

"It doesn't matter," Ryker shook his head. "I just wish I could've done more."

"Ryker, please, no… I love you," I assured him.

"I love you, too. More than you could ever imagine," Ryker said as more tears streamed down his cheeks. "But I know you needed so much more than I could give you. Belle, everything about you amazes me, and you, especially you, never deserved any of the pain you went through.

"I could've done more. I could've been there for you more, I could've showed you more love, I could've kept you from getting injured all the time. And I wanted to be everything you needed. I wanted to make up for your pain. I wanted to save you, believe me, I did. But I... I couldn't."

Ryker continued to cry. "You told me I was more than enough, and I've been trying to live up to that, but I... I just... I can't live up to what you need from me. I wanted to be enough, but I can't, and I'm sorry. I'm so sorry. And now I'm about to lose you, and I... I'm sorry I was never enough for you."

"Ryker," I said weakly, "you... you don't have to be enough. I love you... for who you are... not... not what you've done."

"Please, please don't leave me," Ryker begged.

"You... you have to look after the crew now," I struggled to say.

"I need you."

"I... know... but you... you have to be strong... for me," I pleaded as I dug my face into Ryker's vest. I didn't have much time left.

"Please."

"I can't stay with you forever… You have to let me go," I whispered.

"I can't."

"You have to," I looked up at Ryker, my heart filled with sorrow and shattered to pieces.

"I'll always love you," Ryker held my hand one last time.

I coughed and faintly said, "I love you, too."

We looked at each other with two broken hearts and tears running down our cheeks. We leaned toward each other with the searing pain of saying 'goodbye.' And as we kissed, I closed my eyes for the very last time.

Come Back For Me

A few minutes went by. The minutes turned into hours. The hours turned into days. I was oblivious to life, itself. I was positive I was dead. I was unaware of anything around me... until I heard a voice.

"I mean, I know I tell you I need you just about every day... and, I mean, maybe it's all just stupid. But... I really and truly need you. When I met you, I knew there was something about you that made you different than any other girl I've ever met. And then I realized how beautiful and good-natured and brave you were, and I loved you for it. I'd never met a warrior with the face of a princess like you. You just... you were too wonderful to die, and my heart shattered when I saw the light in you go out.

"You never deserved this. You never deserved anything you went through, ever. And you shouldn't have had to keep apologizing like that. None of this was your fault. I'm the one you should've blamed. I wanted to save you, but all I could do was sit there and feel sorry for you. Not long after, I brought you back here. We tried everything. We bandaged you the best we could, but it's been four days now. Sydney told me you weren't dead, but you were hardly breathing. I told her I wouldn't give up on you, but she said you'd probably never wake up again. If it's all true, and you died, then a piece of me died with you. But if you really are alive, I need you to come back… for me… I need you."

I then realized the voice I'd been hearing *was* real. He only had to say one sentence for me to know it was Ryker. After a minute I realized he was talking to *me*. I felt Ryker's hand holding mine, and the only thing I knew to do in that moment was to curl my fingers around his.

More silence. It was the kind of silence that tries to fill up space when you're waiting for something… something so significant that you don't even know what it is, and all you can do is wait.

I felt two soft fingers brush my hair away from my face. Then that same silence that I thought would never go away. He lifted my head. But I didn't want to wait anymore. I loved Ryker too much to wait. So, I leaned forward and kissed him with all the passion I had in me.

It may have been the most passionate kiss I'd ever experienced. I had never felt so much joy in my life. I finally opened my eyes and looked up at Ryker.

"Well, I… I came back for you," I said as I smiled.

"I thought I'd never see you again," Ryker said with tears in his eyes. He hardly ever showed that much emotion. I rested my head on his shoulder. For a while, neither of us knew what to say. I was overjoyed to see that Ryker's pain was finally going away, along with mine. And in its place, love remained.

"You saved my life," I sniffled.

"You saved mine first."

"I love you."

"I love you, too," Ryker said softly.

"Thank you," I said.

"For what?"

"For never giving up on me," I replied, as I wrapped one of my arms around Ryker.

"You heard that?" Ryker asked.

"Ryker, I..." I didn't know what to say and suddenly broke into tears.

"I don't deserve you," I sobbed. "You've always been so good to me... and I... I love you... I just..."

"Just leave it at that. I love you, too," Ryker interrupted. "Calm down. You need to rest."

"I'm fine," I argued, as I tried to sit up.

"Belle, you were shot, lost part of your right shoulder, and lost a... No, you're not fine," Ryker objected.

"Lost a *what?*" I asked.

"Oh... nothing," Ryker said awkwardly.

"Ryker, I didn't lose anything," I told him. "Oh, did I mention my ring finger's numb?"

"About that…"

"What about it?"

I looked at my left hand and squealed. My finger wasn't *numb*. It was *gone*.

"I… did not expect *that*," I gasped.

"Don't freak out," Ryker begged as he looked away. "Change the subject."

"You're just sad because now there's nowhere to put my wedding ring," I joked.

"No… it's just… I'm not used to that… yet," Ryker stammered.

"How's Dylan?" I asked as I put my hand back under the blanket.

"He's okay. We're letting him room with us," Ryker answered. "But it's Michael I'm worried about. I think Clark scared him. He won't tell us what's wrong."

"Did he ever get the jewels?"

"A few, but..."

"Oh my gosh!" I interrupted. "I just remembered... Clark stabbed you!"

"I'm fine. Don't worry about me," Ryker urged.

"I'm so sorry. I should've stopped him. Really, I really am sorry, really," I said, as I tried to sit up again. I decide to lie back down when I realized sitting up would be too painful.

"It's not your fault. I'm okay. You did the right thing," Ryker reassured me.

Suddenly, my door burst open and in came Sydney, looking madder than ever.

The Secret Unfolds

"Ryker, I can't believe Belle woke up and you didn't even bother to tell me!" Sydney stormed.

"Yeah, yeah, shame on me. I'll leave," Ryker decided.

"You've had your time, now get out and leave us alone," Sydney demanded.

"Don't worry, Belle. I'll be back," Ryker said as he left.

"I'm so glad you're okay," Sydney said, as she awkwardly hugged me.

"Sydney, you can hug me like a normal human," I joked.

"I'm trying not to hurt you. You're crippled. You almost died," Sydney argued.

"I heard Michael's not doing so great. What happened?" I asked.

"I don't know, he won't talk to me," Sydney sighed. "I think Clark said something to him when they were fighting. You know, to get in his head."

"That's what he's best at," I said.

"I mean, you know I'm bad at sympathizing with people, but I actually feel really bad for him," Sydney admitted.

"Oh, wow! You actually have a soul!" I exclaimed.

"You know, you should be nicer to me, since I'm injured."

"You're not injured."

"You wouldn't understand anyway," Sydney sniffled as she dried her tears. "And it's... it's hard to recover when you've lost something that mattered to you more than all the gold in the world."

"What did you lose?" I asked sarcastically.

"My… my nail," Sydney sobbed.

"Oh, you have got to be kidding me," I scoffed. "Your *nail?*"

"Why don't you care?"

"Because I lost a whole finger," I said grimly.

"Fingers aren't as important."

"There's the door!" I ordered.

"You know, when you're friend's in pain, you should care!" Sydney yelled.

"Yeah, Sydney, you should," I returned.

"I don't have too feel bad for you! You're practically my sister!"

"Sydney, do I look anything look anything like your sister?" I asked.

"No, 'cause I'm ugly. My hair's all matted because I slept funny last night, and I have acne. So, no," Sydney answered.

"Your hair looks fine and all girls your age have acne," I argued.

"Not you."

"No, instead I have nine fingers."

"Well, yeah, but it looks all cool and edgy. I just look dumb," Sydney sighed.

"Shut up. You're gorgeous," I said.

"Belle!" I suddenly heard Ginger screamed as she ran to hug me and began to cry. "I was so scared that you died."

"Oh, please, if she was gonna die, she would've been eaten by a shark or something," Sawyer said, as he and Alice followed Ginger.

"Yeah, Sawyer, I *was* almost eaten by a shark, thanks to you," I retorted.

"Yeah, but now you have a great story to tell, right?" Sawyer said with a forced grin. "Right, Belle?"

"You almost killed her," Alice scoffed. "Ginger, scoot over. Let me hug her."

"Be careful," Sydney pleaded. "Don't choke her. Don't crack her ribs. Just please be careful."

"Move it, Ginger," Alice demanded, as she shoved Ginger away and hugged me. "Belle, am I your favorite?"

"I don't have favorites," I replied.

"Ryker's her favorite," Sydney said bluntly.

"Does it hurt where the bullet is?" Sawyer asked.

"What do you think?" I asked sarcastically.

"Does your missing finger hurt?" he asked.

"Sawyer, I can't feel it. It's not there," I retorted.

"Oh, well, then. Since you're crippled, I guess I'll have to be captain," Sawyer decided.

"I'm still captain," I objected.

"But why?" Sawyer whined.

"Sawyer, you have the maturity of a five-year-old. No," I answered.

"I'm telling Ryker," Sawyer said as he began to leave.

"Hey, tell those three to come up here," I told him.

"Fine," Sawyer groaned as he left.

"Belle, we can't have a crew meeting if you can't get up," Sydney argued.

"We'll just have it from here," I said. A few minutes late, Ryker, Sawyer, Michael, and Dylan walked in.

"Belle, I can't believe you're making this poor innocent kid date you," Dylan scolded.

"Am I really that bad?" I asked angrily.

"You cry too much. It's annoying. Yes," he said.

"No she doesn't! She's most amazing and beautiful girl alive! And she's taken, so back off," Ryker said.

"Take her, I don't want her," Dylan admitted.

"Good," Ryker grumbled.

"What's this?" Sawyer asked, as he picked up my mother's diary. "And who's Jacob? Wait. Listen to this.

Do all girls get butterflies when they talk to real men?"

"Sawyer, put that down right now!" I demanded.

"You have *two* exes? Dylan *and* Jacob?" Sawyer inquired.

"Dylan's not my ex, and that's not even my diary," I argued.

"Ha! You're lying!" Sawyer declared.

"Sawyer, that's my mother's," I explained.

"What else is in here?" Sawyer asked himself.

"Put it back!" I ordered. Sawyer put the diary back on my desk.

"Why's Belle's room better than everyone else's?" Dylan asked.

"Because I'm the captain. Don't touch anything. Sydney, why are you trying on my shoes?" I exclaimed.

"Can I keep them?" Sydney begged. "You won't be walking for a while, so…"

"No," I said sharply. "Now, can I please just say what I need to say and get this over with?"

"Sure," Sawyer answered.

"Michael, what are you gonna do with the jewels when you get back to London?" I asked.

"What?" Michael asked. His mind was obviously somewhere else.

"The jewels," I repeated.

"What about them?" he asked.

"What are you gonna do with them?" I asked again.

"Oh… just give them to the king… or someone," Michael said at length.

"Will you be staying with us or going back to your mother?" I asked.

"Which is safer?"

"I thought you were over that."

"Over what?"

"Safety," I answered.

"Well… not anymore. My… no, Clark's probably after me," Michael said awkwardly.

"He was after me. He doesn't care about the jewels. Plus, he can't fight you because he only has one leg. Why would he want you, anyway?"

"Because I'm his… You know, I'd really rather not talk about this," Michael objected.

"You're his *what*?" I asked.

"It's not your concern. I've been through too much already. Leave me alone," Michael began to raise his voice.

"*You* have been through nothing!" I yelled. "Clark has done nothing to you! You should be glad your not me, or Dylan, or his son!"

"Shut up!" Michael shouted.

"Belle, leave him alone," Sydney demanded.

"Michael, are you crying?" I retorted.

"Stop provoking him!" Sydney yelled.

"I'm leaving," Michael decided, as he walked out of my room and slammed the door behind him.

"Leave him alone next time," Sydney said as she left to find Michael. She found him on the deck and said. "Don't listen to her. She just thinks she gets special treatment because she's crippled."

"She's not the only one that almost died," Michael said grimly.

"Why'd that trigger you so much?" Sydney asked. "Clark was never after you, especially not now."

"I really… don't want to talk about that," Michael said timidly.

"I mean, you've just been so distant the past few days. I'm getting worried," Sydney admitted.

"I'm fine."

"I'm gonna miss you," Sydney sighed, "when you go back to London."

Michael stared off into the sea and gave no answer.

"I get it," Sydney continued. "You belong in London, and I belong here. We'll see each other again, someday. I'm sure your mother and father miss you terribly."

"Don't speak of my father," Michael said abruptly.

"Why not?"

"Just don't," Michael replied, his voice shaking.

"You good?" Sydney asked.

"For now," Michael turned to leave.

"What did Sir Phillip ever do to you?" Sydney asked as she followed Michael.

"Phillip never did anything to me!" Michael yelled.

"Then why's he such a pain to talk about?" Sydney went on.

"Phillip has nothing to do with this!" Michael shouted.

"But you said not to talk about your father!" Sydney screamed.

"Shut up, Sydney!" Michael snapped.

"But Phillip..."

"Phillip isn't even my real father!" Michael cried as tears began to stream down his face. "Just leave me alone."

"Who is it, then?" Sydney asked quietly.

"Clark Teach," Michael admitted faintly. "The... the man who tried to kill me... because I'm weak."

"You're not weak," Sydney told Michael. "You fought him off."

"Ryker fought him off," Michael corrected.

"You're still brave," Sydney said as she held Michael's hand, "and I love you for that."

"I love you more," Michael returned, as he smiled for the first time since the day he saw his real father.

A few hours passed and Sydney eventually returned to me. She kicked my door open and frantically said, "Michael is Clark's son. Tell me everything you know."

"Sydney, how dumb do you think I am?" I scoffed.

"Three out of ten. But I'm telling the truth. I need to know what happened to Clark's son," Sydney pleaded.

"Oh... okay," I sighed, not knowing where to start. "So Clark's wife had twins in January of 1680. One was a lot smaller than the other, so Clark decided he was useless and wanted to kill the baby and his mother. The mother and her child escaped, but she got her hand cut off. She then hid in the cargo hold and took care of Dylan for most of that time. When Clark and his crew moved to a bigger ship, his wife and son escaped. But if his son really is Michael, I'm never gonna be able to see him the same way ever again."

Sydney stared at me for a few moments and said, "I don't think he'll ever be able to see himself the same again, either. It's really hard on him. But it all makes so much sense. That's why Michael's step-father hates pirates. That's why his parents are so protective. That's why Michael's smaller than other boys his age, and it also explains why Diane can't move her hand!"

"Because she doesn't have one!" I exclaimed. "I knew it! I was right! I was right this whole time!"

"Oh my gosh," Sydney gasped. "That's the reason you thought Michael was Clark when you threw a sword at him."

"This whole time, I thought I was crazy," I said. "Every time I looked at him, it just gave me this uneasy feeling. I had no idea it was Clark."

"They have a lot of resemblance."

"Yeah."

"Well, I'm sorry to bother you with all this. I'll let you rest now," Sydney said as she left.

"Yeah, you do that," I agreed. The door closed and I was alone. I was finally at peace with myself.

I hadn't the slightest idea how I'd survived. Hardly anyone could defeat Clark, so how had I, of all people, made it out alive? I was just a young girl. Any other girl would have been completely insignificant to Clark.

Then I remembered I wasn't just a young girl. No. I was a miracle. Everything I'd ever been through was impossible. A girl like me defeating Clark was impossible. But I was strong enough, and that strength had come from God the moment I realized He had a plan.

I was thankful to be alive. Even more, I was thankful for the fact that I never had to be afraid... no matter what.

Where Dreams Set Sail

The days went by slowly. The weather was fair and the seas were calm. I let Ryker run the ship for me, since it still hurt too much to walk. He would constantly come and talk to me. He'd ask me how I was for the fifth time that day and hold my injured hand until there was some other job for him to do. He worked every hour he was awake and when he wasn't working, he was with me.

"You need to stop working so much," I said one day.

"I'm fine," Ryker countered.

"Make Sawyer do it. He needs discipline," I replied.

"I was just gonna tell you we're almost in London," he said.

"Oh, that was fast," I said. "It's only been a week."

"Yeah. The weather was good. No people getting struck by lightning, or freezing to death, or anything like that," Ryker said.

"Just as long as there's no one trying to wrestle a shark, I'm good," I joked.

"I'm surprised that psycho hasn't been put in a nut house by now," Ryker scoffed.

"Yeah," I agreed. "So, how much longer till London?"

"A few hours," Ryker replied.

"I feel so bad for Sydney. Michael's leaving her. He thinks he'll be safer in London," I sighed.

"Look, as long as he's nowhere near Sydney, he's safe," Ryker said.

"Yeah, but they were actually doing really good. She needs him," I argued.

"What she needs is a…" Ryker lowered his voice, "a *therapist.*"

"Why are we being so quiet?" I whispered.

"Did somebody say *therapist?*" Sawyer exclaimed as he barged into my room.

"Go away," Ryker grumbled.

"Michael wants you to help him get his stuff to take to London," Sawyer said.

"Fine," Ryker said as he stood up. "I'll be back later."

"Have fun," I joked as he left.

I tried to rest for the next few hours. I wasn't in nearly as much pain as before, but it still hurt too much to sleep. My right arm couldn't move, not to mention part of my shoulder had been cut off. My left ring finger was gone. It hurt to breathe, and I still couldn't walk because my legs had been cut so badly. Every day I would wake up and convince myself I would recover, but deep down, I worried I'd never be the same.

Later that day, Ryker carried me out to the deck. The whole crew was waiting there for Michael's departure.

"Goodbye, Michael," I said curtly. "Have fun with your overprotective parents. And just so you know, I don't hate you anymore. Having the courage to fight Clark makes you a lot less pathetic... and... yeah, that's it."

"Thank you all for giving me a chance," Michael said. I rolled my eyes at his cliché little speech.

"I'll miss you dearly, and I hope to see you all some time again," Michael went on. "Now, if I could speak with Sydney alone... please."

"Sure," I said. "Sydney, untie the ship after he leaves so we can get out of here."

Sydney nodded. As the crew dispersed, Sydney walked over to Michael and quietly said, "It's okay that you're leaving. I'm not a very good person to be around. I appreciate you. For a few weeks, I actually had someone to love. And I... I know that love doesn't last very long at our age. I'm just glad someone actually noticed me for once."

"That's actually why I wanted to speak with you," Michael admitted. "I want you to come with me."

"No," Sydney sniffled. "I can't. Not London. Never London."

"Why not?" Michael asked.

"Because London brings back too many bad memories," Sydney replied. "It makes me question my worth. I know you don't understand. Don't worry. You don't have to. I won't burden you with the complexity of my mind. My father always told me I was wired different."

"'Wired?'" Michael repeated.

"You know, like in computers and stuff," Sydney explained.

"I don't even know what that is," Michael said.

"Me neither. I'm just making a point. You don't have to understand me," Sydney said.

"Well, then, I have a confession. I don't understand you, at all. You're the most complicated girl I've ever met, and I love you for that. Because the truth is, you're a mystery to me sometimes, and I find it beautiful."

"If we're being completely honest, I have a confession, too," Sydney admitted. "I really, really don't want you to leave. There's no one else out there like you. But I know you can't stay. We all have to wake up from dreaming at some point, right? But I love you, more than I can explain."

"I love you, too," Michael said. Both remained silent, with no words left to say. After one last kiss, Sydney and Michael let go of each other and Michael walked into the harbor.

He stood at the edge of the dock and froze before the streets of London. He looked out into the city, ready to go back to his ordinary life.

Suddenly, Michael dropped the queen's jewels, along with everything he owned. He turned toward the *Pegasus* and began to run back to Sydney. He embraced her at the dock and spun her around in his arms. Sydney broke into tears, as she whispered, "I love you."

"I'm never leaving you again," Michael promised.

"We should get married!" Sydney exclaimed.

"*Now?*" Michael retorted.

"No! I mean when we're like, twenty!" Sydney laughed.

"Oh," Michael sighed. "Okay. That... that's better."

"But... what about the palace, and your stuff, and everything you took with you?" Sydney asked.

"I don't want it anymore," Michael decided. "That life is worth nothing without you."

"Why do people always fall in love at this harbor?" Sydney asked.

"Because this is the harbor where dreams set sail," Michael answered. "You aimlessly wait and dream for someone to love you, and then the mist in the air, the music of the sea, it changes you. It's the threshold between courage and safety. And when you have the courage to fall in love, you finally let go of the supposed 'safety' that held you back. Because sometimes, what looks like safety is really just fear."

"Well, I'm not afraid to love you anymore," Sydney told Michael.

"Me neither."

And at that, Sydney kissed Michael, with trust, in place of fear. Michael took Sydney back to the *Pegasus* as the sun set behind them. He untied the rope that kept the ship from drifting away, as though he were untying the last knot that kept him safe in London.

$\mathcal{F}_{ree}$

The sky grew darker as the hours went by. I remained in my room most of the evening, until I heard an overly loud knock at my door.

"Belle! We're about to have supper if you wanna come!" Alice screamed.

"Alice!" Ginger scolded. "She's probably trying to rest."

"No, I'm just bored," I corrected. "And the door's unlocked, by the way."

"Well, then!" Alice kicked open the door. "Are you gonna eat with us, or not?"

"I mean, I can't really get up," I replied. " So, no."

"Why don't you just let Ryker help you?" Ginger asked.

"Yeah, Belle, he *loves* acting like the man we all know he's not," Alice added.

"Ryker's the only man on this ship," I argued.

"What about Dylan?" Alice taunted.

"Alright, Alice, you really need to stop acting like Dylan was my boyfriend," I begged.

"Why?" Alice asked.

"Because he's practically my brother," I retorted.

"*Ewwww!*" Alice shrieked. "You dated your brother?"

"No, that's not what she said," Ginger corrected.

"Are you going to eat supper, or not?" Alice asked again.

I sighed. "Sure."

"Okay," Ginger said, as she and Alice ran to find Ryker. A few minutes later, Ryker came in. He carried me to the couch and gently set me down. Ryker then moved the table closer to me and sat down next to me.

"You didn't have to move the table just for me," I said.

"No, I don't mind," Ryker said. "As long as you're comfortable, I'll do whatever you want."

"You're my boyfriend, not my servant," I argued.

"Same thing," Ryker said.

"I wish I could pay you back, somehow," I sighed.

"Just… stop trying to get yourself killed," Ryker begged.

"Okay, okay," I agreed. "I'll try."

"Hey, look who's crying on Ryker's shoulder again," Sawyer scoffed as he came to the table.

"Shut up, Sawyer," Sydney snapped, as the rest of the crew came behind her.

"Hey, why do you get to sit next to her?" Alice whined.

"Because I'm her boyfriend," Ryker bragged.

"You're a bully," Alice pouted.

"You're a red-headed leprechaun," Ryker returned.

"Thank you!" Alice exclaimed. "Red-heads are very attractive, unlike you."

"Alice, sit down," I interrupted. "Wait a minute. Michael, why are *you* here?"

"Because I have a better boyfriend than you," Sydney answered.

"*Squawk!* Yeah!" Donna agreed. "Both of them!"

"Both?" Sawyer laughed.

"Yeah! *Squawk!* Michael and Jerry!" Donna replied.

"Jerry's my pet, not my boyfriend," Sydney retorted.

"Jerry's gonna give us all the Black Plague," Ryker scoffed. "Michael, whatever you do, do not kiss that rat-lover."

"Too late," Michael said with a grin.

"Jerry is a ferret!" Sydney yelled. "You're gonna hurt his feelings."

Jerry squeaked and nodded his head in agreement.

"He's a ferret," Dylan said. "He doesn't have feelings."

"If I were you, I'd shut up so I don't get punched," Sydney threatened.

"Oh, I'm so scared of getting punched by a girl!" Dylan said sarcastically.

"You should be," Alice warned. "I can punch a grown man hard enough to make him cry. I'm really great at boxing, kung-fu, wrestling, jiu-jitsu, krav-maga, karate, sword fighting…"

"Yeah, that's really believable coming from a five-year-old," Dylan scoffed.

"She's eight!" Sawyer screamed.

"Sawyer, calm down," Michael said with a laugh.

"I was wrong about you. Belle's too good for you," Alice said.

"Wow, Dylan, you're so good at first impressions," I said, as I rolled my eyes.

"Maybe you should be nicer to the only one who ever took care of you," Dylan said.

"What about my boyfriend?" I said, grinning.

"Ryker, why do you look... entertained?" Sydney asked.

"Oh, 'cause seeing Belle and Dylan act like they hate each other comforts him," Sawyer answered.

"Wait, what?" Ryker shrieked.

"I mean, it's pretty obvious that you're jealous of Dylan," Sawyer went on.

"No, I'm not!" Ryker yelled.

"It's okay, Ryker. Sydney was jealous of Belle," Sawyer added.

"Why would you be jealous of Belle?" Dylan laughed.

"Because she's pretty," Sydney replied.

"No, she's not," Dylan said.

"Alright, that's it!" Ryker yelled as he stood up.

"Ryker, it's okay, sit down," I said. "He didn't mean anything by it."

"Belle, I can't just sit here and watch him insult you," Ryker argued.

"Sure, Belle's decent. Fine," Dylan decided.

"She's gorgeous," Ryker grumbled as he sat down.

"Hey, if you guys could please shut up for five minutes, I have something I need to say to all of you," I announced.

"*Squawk!* Me, too!" Donna exclaimed.

"Not right now," I said quickly.

"You're treating me like some animal, and I don't like it!" Donna squawked.

"I mean," Michael started, "you are..."

"Anyway," I interrupted, " I just wanted to thank all of you for what you did the other day. I know that I'm usually the one dragging you into all of my crazy problems. But you guys could have died out there, and I'm sure you all knew that. The fact that you were all willing to fight for me means a lot. So thank you. All of you. And I know that God must have kept me alive with a miracle, but you all were brave enough to be a part of it. And because of you guys, I'm free."

"You're welcome," Sawyer said casually.

"Sawyer, you didn't even do anything," Alice retorted.

"I'd almost die for your shenanigans any day," Sawyer said proudly.

"Yeah, I mean, you were always there for us," Sydney added.

"We had to help you," Alice said. "We're your family."

The word 'family' echoed through my mind over and over. I had never had a family before. Ryker had always been the only person I could ever depend on. Then I realized that a family was more than just the people you're related to. It's the people you love.

"Ryker's your family?" Sawyer exclaimed.

"No!" I screamed.

"I don't count! I'm her boyfriend!" Ryker yelled.

"*Squawk!* Sawyer, you're the stupidest, most idiotic idiot I have ever met!" Donna screeched.

"Donna, you can't even be talking right now," Sydney said.

"Well, at least I don't get mad at everyone when my hair gets in my face!" Donna replied.

"At least I have hair!" Sydney returned.

"*Squawk!* I'm going to my cage!" Donna stormed as she flew into my room.

"It is getting pretty late," Ginger said.

"Yeah, and it's freezing out here," Sydney complained. "Plus, Jerry needs help with his skin care."

Jerry squeaked happily.

"He probably has fleas," Ryker commented.

"Rodents are actually very sanitary, unlike you," Sydney said as she got up to leave. "Goodnight."

"Michael, you've literally said nothing this whole time," Ryker said.

"I'm just tired from everything that's happened lately," Michael replied. "I was about to call it a day."

"Are you staying for good?" Ryker asked.

"Yes, actually. This is my home now," Michael said, as he left the table.

"Good," Ryker said. "I was afraid you were gonna leave me with those psychos."

"Hey, Michael," I added. "Thanks for not being a chicken."

"Thanks for not treating me like one," Michael said, just before he went below deck.

Soon after that, everyone else began to leave, and I was left alone with Ryker. I looked up at the night sky, which was shining brighter than ever, and there was a very rare moment of peace that night.

"You know, we never had stars like this in the city," Ryker said.

"Really?" I asked quietly.

"Yeah," Ryker said. "The buildings always blocked them out. I mean, there were a few, but nothing like this."

"Did you like the city?"

"Oh, no," Ryker answered. "I hated it. It was too crowded, and everyone had these really ugly wigs. And there were always people yelling at each other. Everyone had everything, but they were never happy. They wanted to buy happiness with money. But you know what the worst part was?"

"What?"

"Not having you with me," Ryker said as he smiled at me.

"When I was living on the *Cobra*, the one thing I always wanted was for some really cute boy to come and rescue me, and take me away with him," I admitted. "I never thought that would actually happen."

"You rescued me first," Ryker said.

"Yeah, just so that you could tolerate how emotional I am," I joked.

"I don't just tolerate you. I love you," Ryker countered.

"Well, everyone else has to tolerate me," I argued.

"Yeah, right. You're the most admired girl I've ever met," Ryker said. "You're smart, and pretty, and fearless..."

"I'm not fearless," I interrupted. "Believe me, I was scared to death when I was about to fight Clark. I just decided to put my fear aside because it was getting in my way. Being afraid just wasn't helping."

"I don't think I ever thanked you... for saving my life," Ryker confessed.

"You don't have to thank me," I said, as I looked up at him. "I should be thanking you."

"I was just doing what any decent person would do," Ryker said.

"No, even decent people would have given up on me by now. I promise, there's no one out there like you. You never have to save my life, you just do," I said, as my eyes welled up with tears.

"No, I have to," Ryker said as he dried my tears. "I could never imagine life without you. And after everything we've been through together, I promise I'll be there every second you need me. I'll even be there when you don't need me."

"I'll always need you," I sniffled. "I love you more than I could ever explain."

"I love you, too," Ryker said as he wrapped his arm around my shoulder.

"But you really didn't have to go through all that trouble for me. I already know you love me. You don't have to prove that," I said.

"Yes, I did," Ryker countered, "because the people who actually love you don't just stand there and watch you suffer. They suffer with you until you're free."

I didn't know what to say. Ryker had shown me a type of love that some people don't even know exists. True love. It's the kind of love that's painted on your heart and can't be washed away. It's a hand that you can never let go of. Sometimes, true love is just a few sweet words you can never forget, even if you tried.

"Ryker," I said quietly, "you'll always be the one for me."

"And you'll always be mine," Ryker promised. We looked into each other's eyes, both knowing that our love was permanent. I leaned closer to him. The perfection of this moment was too beautiful to be wasted.

I had gone on the journey prepared for me. I had won back justice from Clark. I had almost died in the process. My pain was over. I had run out of reasons to worry. I was finally free from my anxiety. And I was grateful for it.

I looked at Ryker with relief and joy. I was safe. I was free. I was going to spend forever with the love of my life.

I closed my eyes. My mind went back to the day I met him. I thought about all the times he had saved my life. Every word he'd ever said to me echoed in my heart. We had been through so much together, and there was more to come. But I knew I was safe with Ryker. I knew I could trust him. I remembered our first kiss. I remembered every tear, every scream, every laugh, and every smile. But after those few seconds, my thoughts flooded away completely as Ryker kissed me.

Also from

Eliza Crooks

and

Grace Under Pressure Publishing

The Voyage of the Pegasus

(the first book in the series)

Stay tuned for more, as

The Return of the Cobra

promises yet more story to come!

Visit graceunderpressure.com for more information.